The
SCOTUS
Affair

The
SCOTUS
Affair

A Dimase Augustin Thriller

STEPHEN L BRUNEAU

THE SCOTUS AFFAIR
A DIMASE AUGUSTIN THRILLER

iUniverse books may be ordered through booksellers or by contacting:

iUniverse
1663 Liberty Drive
Bloomington, IN 47403
www.iuniverse.com
1-800-Authors (1-800-288-4677)

ISBN: 978-1-5320-9974-8 (sc)
ISBN: 978-1-6632-0200-0 (hc)
ISBN: 978-1-5320-9973-1 (e)

Library of Congress Control Number: 2020907861

Print information available on the last page.

iUniverse rev. date: 05/23/2020

Dedicated to my Mother and Father, who instilled a love of reading and writing in me from an early age.

CHAPTER 1

Boston, Massachusetts: Present Day

Ben Johnson stood alone in the middle of the Boston Common with his arms outstretched and his gaze directed toward the sky. It was a bright, warm July morning, and he could feel the heat of the sun on his upturned face. A solitary tear meandered down his cheek, cutting a random path before dripping onto the front of his shirt.

But no one would notice. The park below was full of people. He watched them in the distance from atop a grassy knoll, away from the crowded paths. No one paid him any mind, and anyone who happened to pass by was oblivious to his presence.

Ben Johnson was a good man, one who made an effort to treat others fairly. He did not believe life was a zero-sum game. He did not believe that for his business to prosper, others had to suffer. To the contrary, his business formula was to enhance the lives of others—to build transformative value, to create or improve. He believed that relationships were the key to success, and he surrounded himself with people who had the same energies. On the foundation of that philosophy, he had become one of the wealthiest black entrepreneurs in the country.

In contrast, Ben also found that when wealth or power was inherited, the deeper into the generational tree that inheritance occurred, the greater the propensity for a sense of entitlement. That condition was not ubiquitous, but often, those who were handed great value didn't understand or appreciate what it had taken to build that value. Worse, when push came to shove, they might be willing to do anything to hold on to it. When one encountered an issue of corruption, a sense of entitlement was often the basis for it. Corruption begot corruption, and thus was the yin and the yang of the business world.

None of that mattered to Ben Johnson in the current moment. He thought he felt his phone vibrate and put his hand near his pocket. It was still. He let out a ragged breath. The phone call he'd received earlier had shaken him to his core. The two of them had discussed exactly that type of situation in the past, but those conversations always had been in the abstract, about a hypothetical event in the distant future, not about something real. Now the unthinkable had happened. His world had turned upside down, and he was helpless to change it.

The love of his life was dying, lying in a coma fifteen hundred miles away, and there wasn't a damn thing he could do about it.

◆　◆　◆

The call had come from her sister, Amandine. Acadia had made arrangements for her sister to contact him in the unlikely event of just such a scenario. Otherwise, how would he have known? Of course, he eventually would have found out, but letting her sister in on their little secret and having her perform the task certainly had spared him days of uncertainty and anguish.

If the situation had been reversed and he had gone a day without contacting her, she could have simply called his office, and someone would have informed her if he was sick or hurt or worse. Things were not as straightforward with her. The presence of a husband and two adult kids dictated that. At age seventy, she no longer had an office for him to call.

Ben and Acadia were the same age, and they'd first met almost forty years and $50 billion worth of developed properties ago. Now, at age seventy, Ben was the senior managing partner of and majority shareholder in Fischer, Forbes, and Johnson. From a career standpoint, he had been on a rocket ship his entire life. By every measure, he was a man to be admired and envied, but he didn't feel that way that day.

Acadia LaFleur and Ben had been an improbable couple back then: he had been an ambitious young black businessman from the North, and she had been a beautiful white Cajun princess of the South. He, despite his young age, had been a sophisticated, college-educated powerbroker, moving easily among the rich and powerful, a city boy through and through. She, a southern belle in a world of deep tradition, had never been out of Louisiana, and her family's position was rooted in nepotism and local political power.

The flood of memories was overwhelming.

◆　◆　◆

The first time Ben ever laid eyes on her was an accident of fate. The meeting was scheduled with her father-in-law, who happened to be the mayor of Alexandria, Louisiana, a growing city on the banks of the Red River of the South. Ben did not expect anyone else to be at the meeting.

Ben had never been to Alexandria. He was only thirty at the time, and his boss at Fischer and Forbes assigned him to fly down and feel out the mayor regarding the possibility of building a hotel and convention complex and a river walk. Ben was excited about the opportunity. It was to be a significant project, and if he pulled it off, it would be a major feather in his cap.

The mayor, Clement LaFleur, was at least thirty years Ben's senior and was a political animal if ever there was one. He was a professional politician, and as it turned out, politics was the family business. Just as some folks were born into farming or the real estate business, the mayor was the third in his family to hold the position; his father and grandfather had served before him in an unbroken chain of succession dating back to the turn of the previous century.

Ben and the mayor sat at a small conference table in the center of the mayor's formidable office, when she made her entrance. Both men rose as the mayor made formal introductions.

"Mr. Johnson, this is Miss Acadia LaFleur. She is officially our ambassador of goodwill here in Alexandria. She also happens to be my daughter-in-law, a fact that makes her uniquely qualified for the job."

The mayor chuckled at his own reference to nepotism as he politely pulled out a chair for Acadia. She was an extraordinarily beautiful woman but not in a self-conscious way. She extended her hand toward Ben, and he lightly grasped her fingers. They were delicate and perfectly manicured in a flattering, subtle pink that offset her pink-and-white flower-print dress. Ben forced himself to let go. He felt as if a faint electrical current had passed briefly between them when they touched. He couldn't recall ever having felt anything quite like it in the past. He was momentarily thrown off his game.

The mayor was speaking, and Ben nodded politely, only half hearing what he said. Ben wasn't used to being distracted, particularly in a business meeting. He prided himself on his skill set in meetings like that one, particularly on his ability to make the other person feel as if he or she were the most important person in his world, the sole focus of his undivided attention. It was a trait that was effective with friend and foe alike.

Ben subtly turned his head back and forth between the mayor and his daughter-in-law, trying to make it appear that he was including them both in the conversation and making eye contact with each of them. It wasn't going well. His body movements and mannerisms were on automatic pilot, the product of hundreds of such meetings, but his brain kept telling him, *Look at her again. Look at her again.*

Acadia sat across from him, smiling demurely, while the mayor did all the talking. Her raven hair was shoulder length, and her face was classic, with just a hint of Native American, as evidenced by her high cheekbones and light olive skin. Her legs were crossed in a ladylike pose, and she leaned slightly forward in her chair, as if Ben were the only person in the room. That was supposed to be his technique, but her presence had turned the tables on him.

Her cotton dress fell just below her knees. She wore no nylons on her perfectly shaped legs, and her skin was flawless. One of her open-toed pink high heels dangled slightly from an elevated foot. Her toes were sleek, with nails trimmed and polished to perfection, matching her fingernails. More than anything, her eyes kept drawing him back; they were dark brown and radiated an energy from within that he found captivating.

Ben's head continued to rotate between the two of them. He felt like a silly schoolboy, with a frozen smile plastered on his face. He was uncomfortably self-conscious.

Suddenly, the mayor pushed back his chair, extending his hand once again.

"I have to go press some flesh at the Knights of Columbus luncheon. I've asked Acadia to take you around town to take a look at some of the potential sites for our project. That's what a goodwill ambassador does. We like to keep it all in the family around here." He smiled at Acadia, kissed her hand, and then abruptly rushed out of the office, leaving the two of them alone.

CHAPTER
2

For lunch, Acadia selected Crabby Max, a cozy crab shack built partially on the riverbank and extending over the water, supported by a series of pylons. Of course, the establishment was owned by a cousin of some sort. They were shown to a table in the back with a beautiful view of the river. Ben wondered briefly how many goodwill tours Acadia had kicked off with lunch at that same table. Ben had never been in a business meeting quite like that one before. Acadia kept the topic on the potential project, but it was impossible not to feel something different. The proximity of her body, the smell of her perfume, and her easy, unassuming manner and soft laugh were intoxicating.

Ben could have listened to her talk all day. He wished they had ten projects to discuss so the lunch could stretch on for hours. Drinks came, two pale ales, and Acadia declared that after the meal, they would conduct the tour from east to west, following the river as they visited each site.

Acadia ordered a shared crawfish boil for them, referring to the crawfish as mudbugs. For all his experience in five-star restaurants, this was something new. A little tentative at first, he watched, fascinated, as she gave a quick tutorial on the finer points of eating so-called mudbugs. She pulled one from the steaming pile and held it up for him to see. She broke off the head with her delicate fingers, pushed the meat through the tail into her mouth, and then sucked the juices out of the head.

There was something sensual and seductive about the way she did it, though not purposefully. She had a natural confidence but did not seem aware of it. Ben followed suit—at first awkwardly and with some reservation, but he quickly caught on. Acadia smiled and complimented him on how quickly he'd picked up on the nuances. They took their time, eating, chatting, sipping the pale ale, and enjoying the view and each other's company. Ben had never met anyone quite like her. If he could have, he would have frozen time that afternoon.

After lunch, they returned to her powder-blue Lincoln Continental convertible to begin the tour. Ben couldn't place the year but realized the car must have been at least ten years old despite its impeccable condition. With the top down, Acadia drove, and Ben sat beside her in the passenger seat. At each of the three locations, she parked the car, and they got out to walk around. Occasionally, she took him by the hand or arm to guide him this way or that. There were no false pretenses or airs, just two people enjoying time together more than either of them would have thought.

Ben had noticed the wedding ring on her finger back when they'd first met in the mayor's office, and he hadn't missed the fact that the mayor had introduced her as his daughter-in-law. He told himself several times that there was nothing wrong with the fact that he enjoyed her company. It was a business meeting, after all. She was beautiful. She was captivating. He could appreciate those qualities without crossing the line. To do anything else would not have been right. She belonged to someone else, someone he couldn't even picture and whom he knew nothing about.

She had a life—one that had gone on just fine without him for many years. He wondered if she had children. He wondered if her husband was as interesting and charming as she was. *They must be something together,* he thought. *What a lucky fellow he must be.*

At that moment, as they walked down a secluded section of grassy path alongside the river at the third location, she suddenly turned and kissed him. It wasn't a long kiss, at least at first. It was more of a question, as if she were saying, *Is this okay?* He was taken by surprise but didn't resist. Acadia sensed his acceptance and went in for a much longer kiss, hard and full, pulling him tightly to her.

Nothing happened for the rest of that first trip to Alexandria. There was no mad rush back to a hotel room or panting, pawing lovemaking in the backseat of the Lincoln parked on some out-of-the-way road on the bayou. They kissed long and hard, passionately, and then she took his hand and continued the tour as if nothing had occurred.

But everything had changed.

CHAPTER
3

Boston, Massachusetts: Present Day

Ben composed himself and found a public water fountain, where he splashed some water onto his face and then dried his eyes on the sleeve of his shirt. He was as emotional as he'd ever felt; his stomach was nauseous, and his mind randomly flashed through a lifetime of images.

Focus, he told himself. *You have to find out why.*

He walked back toward his car.

As painful as it would have been, he could have accepted a heart attack, a stroke, or some kind of natural illness. At least he would have been able to speak to her at some point and comfort her somehow. This was not like that.

He could not comfort her, speak to her, or ease her pain. Acadia was unconscious, deep in a coma, and according to Amandine, she was within a breath of losing her life. The worst part, the part Ben could not get his head around, was the reason. Acadia was not lying at death's door in a hospital bed because old age had caught up to her. In truth, before the latest turn of events, Acadia had been about as young as a seventy-year-old could have been, looking twenty years younger than her chronological age. Acadia was in her present condition because someone had put her there.

According to Amandine, Acadia had been attacked during a home invasion. Police were puzzled because nothing seemed to be missing, and robbery did not appear to be the motive. There was no sign of forced entry. Acadia had been home alone at the time of the attack. She'd been found at the bottom of the main staircase, near the foyer to the front entrance. She was severely bruised, with a number of broken bones, most likely as a result of falling or being pushed down the stairs.

At first, the authorities thought she might have had a terrible accident, tripping and falling down the stairs, but now they thought something else had happened. She'd suffered various injuries one might have expected from falling down a flight of stairs, but one injury was inconsistent with the others and was most likely the cause of her coma.

"Blunt force trauma to the head" was how the police put it. In plain English, someone had knocked her down the stairs. Either that, or someone had knocked her out and later thrown her down in a deliberate act to cover up the original attack.

Whatever weapon had been used was nowhere to be found. The speculation was that the attacker had taken it when he or she fled. Some blood spatter on the landing at the top of the stairs suggested that was where the blow had been struck.

It was not hard to explain the lack of forced entry. Acadia and her husband, Alphonse, lived in an area where no one locked their doors. Anyone could have come in the back way. The intruder could have come in at any time of day and left the same way. He or she could have waited for hours to ambush Acadia or could have been in and out in five minutes.

Police were busy interviewing servants, gardeners, service people, and anyone else who might have had cause to be at the house, though apparently none had been there at the time of the attack. Alphonse had flown back from Washington, DC, to be at his wife's side. Her children, Babette and Clement II, were also there.

Clement II was now the mayor of Alexandria, and Babette, who was married and had her own family, lived in the area. The LaFleur clan had continued to expand their political power in the decades since Ben first met them during the river walk project. After Clement II's granddad had passed away unexpectedly of a heart attack, Clement's son Francois had been elected mayor in a special election. He'd served as mayor for ten years before expanding his base enough to run for Congress, where he was now in his fourth term.

Throughout Francois's time as mayor and in Congress, his brother, Alphonse, had been at his side—never in the spotlight but always at the center of his brother's inner circle. When Francois had succeeded his father as mayor, Alphonse had been there. When Francois had gone to Washington, so had Alphonse. Not one to be in the public eye, Phonse continued his role as a facilitator, fixer, and liaison for so-called community relations.

Acadia's children, Babette and Clement II, were now ages forty-seven and forty-four, respectively. Back when Uncle Francois had made his transition to the national scene, the family had orchestrated a carefully coordinated effort to install Clement II as the next mayor. There had been an election, of course, but the way politics worked in Alexandria, the election had been a mere formality.

Acadia, for her part, had aged gracefully over the years and slowly transformed into the role of family matriarch, dividing her life between local political and charitable events and family and, on some occasions, finding time to spend with Ben Johnson. She and Alphonse had long since given up the pretense of a loving marriage—not to the outside world but certainly between each other. There was no hatred or animosity, just acceptance that they were largely destined to lead separate lives and tolerance of that circumstance. After all, there were appearances to be kept up for one of the most powerful families in Louisiana.

Ben sighed and opened the car door. Wallowing in grief and self-pity would do nothing to help Acadia. He had made his choices, and he had to live with them. She would always be with him, a huge part of who he was. There was, however, one thing he could do. He resolved to do everything in his power to find out who had done this to the love of his life—and why.

CHAPTER
4

Alexandria, Louisiana: 1978

There was a meeting scheduled at the mayor's office that day. It wasn't a matter of selling the mayor on the project. That was a done deal. The challenge was to sell the mayor on his terms and conditions. The mayor wanted the project to happen as much as Ben did, probably more, as it was a once-in-a-lifetime opportunity to advance the family empire, multiply his fortune, and expand his political power.

The mayor would offer no resistance. Ben knew he might have to tamp down his expectations a little bit. There was enough to go around without the mayor having to gouge everyone on real estate commissions, take bribes, manipulate certain parcels, or monopolize business start-ups at the back end. Ben was realistic enough to know he couldn't control all the mayor's behind-the-scenes activities, but at least on the front end, the mayor would have to accept a pricing formula for offers made to property owners and a standardized 5 percent commission if his son was to be awarded the task of making offers, negotiating terms, and consolidating the acquisitions.

The mayor hemmed and hawed and offered token resistance to some of the conditions Ben imposed, but in the end, he could not look a gift horse in the mouth.

Hands were shaken, and backs were slapped all around. The mayor was in an ebullient mood and declared that a celebration was in order. He invited Ben to his home for cocktails and dinner later that evening, a small affair for about fifty people, including town officials, friends, and family, most of whom were one and the same. Ben wondered if Acadia LaFleur would be invited. He still hadn't determined if she was married to the Realtor son or to one of his siblings. He imagined he'd find out sooner or later.

At the appointed hour, an old dark blue Lincoln Town Car pulled up in front of the Bentley Hotel. Ben was waiting, as instructed. The driver hopped out, ran around the front of the car, and held the rear door open for Ben to slide in. The driver was a young twentysomething with straggly brown hair and a sparse blond beard that couldn't quite establish itself. He was casually dressed, but almost as an afterthought, he had a small chauffeur's cap perched awkwardly atop his head. He grinned into the rearview mirror as they pulled out.

"Uncle Clement said to make sure we on time, so here I is. You that man who's gonna build up the downtown and make us all rich?"

Ben returned the smile. Obviously, the mayor had been broadcasting the good news to his followers. Rather than responding with an economic forecast, Ben merely asked the young man his name.

"Billie Bob Breaux, at your service—head of transportation, handyman, and all-around gofer. Jack of many trades and master of none."

The boy seemed thrilled with his lot in life, and Ben had to admire both his enthusiasm and his self-deprecation.

The youth beamed at Ben through the mirror. "We got about a fifteen-minute drive. You just settle back and relax. Uncle Clement got a beautiful place. Wait till you see it."

The mayor's house did not disappoint. Billie Bob turned off the main route onto a secondary road surrounded by thick growth on both sides. Presently, the growth thinned out, and they turned into a long crushed-gravel driveway lined by mature oak trees on either side. Beyond the trees was at least five acres of open field, and about three hundred yards in, as they rounded a curve, the home came spectacularly into view.

The house was large and white, with a stunning wrap-around porch that ran the entire length of the second floor. The front entrance featured minicolumns, a small portico, and double mahogany doors. The windows were oversized and elaborately trimmed. The driveway circled in front of the house and had a large cutout square to one side, where several vehicles were parked.

Billie Bob pulled directly in front of the entryway steps and hustled around to open the door for Ben. At the top of the steps, a uniformed servant greeted Ben, holding a tray of mint julip cocktails. The man was obviously expecting him.

"Welcome to LaFleur House," the servant said, extending the tray so Ben could take a glass. "The mayor is happy you are here."

Ben nodded and smiled graciously.

Behind the man, a grand staircase curved up to the second floor, to an open hallway with a fancy railing running down the full length of one wall. Past the entryway, the central room opened up to high ceilings that rose all the way through the second story above. Small groupings of people were clustered about the room, engaged in separate conversations. A grand piano sat in one corner, with several formal arrangements of chairs, couches, and small tables filling up the space. Fancy curtains adorned the insides of the windows, and several oil portraits were interspersed on the walls, along with beautiful paintings of the house, grounds, and river. Ben imagined the portraits were of an earlier generation of LaFleurs. He recognized one of the mayor himself.

Straight through from the entrance, a pair of oversized french doors were cast wide open, allowing a view all the way to the river beyond. A huge stone patio transitioned the back of the house to an open yard rolling two or three hundred feet down to the river. In the distance, Ben could see a long wooden dock with several different boats tied to the quay.

All in all, a pretty impressive property, Ben thought. He wondered what a property like that would have cost if built on Cape Cod—clearly, millions of dollars. His guess was that the estate had been in the LaFleur family for generations. Nonetheless, it was a gem and well maintained.

The mayor was holding court with five or six people by the grand piano, when he noticed Ben and broke away to greet him. "Welcome, my friend," he proclaimed, opening his arms wide for a hug despite holding a drink in one hand. "Let me introduce you around."

The mayor took Ben by the arm and escorted him around the room, introducing him to a wide variety of different degrees of cousins, uncles, aunts, nephews, and other sundry friends and associates. Ben shook hands, patted shoulders, and generally matched the mayor step for step in his ability to work the room. At an intimate furniture arrangement in one corner, they came across Acadia and two other women sitting on a couch and matching formal chairs.

"You remember Miss Acadia, of course. She is married to my son Alphonse. You'll meet him too. He's around here somewhere."

Acadia remained seated but extended her hand, which Ben took gently, and bowing, he kissed the top of her fingers. He felt the current again but forced it from his thoughts.

"This is her younger sister, Amandine. She is also a LaFleur now, married to my other son, Francois. He's the Realtor. You have to meet him as well. And this young lady over here is their cousin Anne-Marie."

The other women also extended their hands, and Ben kissed each of them in turn. He would have liked to linger for some small talk, but the mayor pulled him along by the elbow. "Come out back to the patio. That's where the bar's set up. We have to get you a real drink."

Ben cast a glance back over his shoulder as the mayor dragged him away. Acadia's eyes met his for a brief instant, and then she turned to resume the conversation with her companions.

The patio was expansive. On one side, two bartenders were busy pouring, surrounded by a half dozen men holding drinks in hand and loudly bantering back and forth. On the other side, two long tables were arranged end to end, covered with hors d'oeuvres.

The crowd at the bar parted as the mayor and Ben approached. "What will you have?" the mayor asked. "Grab a drink, and I'll introduce you to the boys." He waved his arm.

Ben was not a huge drinker, but he understood symbolism in a situation like that. He would pace himself. It was not a crowd in which to order a wine spritzer if one was concerned with first impressions.

"Southern Comfort on the rocks, please," Ben said.

The mayor slapped him on the back and turned him around. "These here are my two sons. Francois is the Realtor I've been telling you about. I'm sure you two will be working together a lot. He's married to Amandine, who you met inside, and this is Alphonse. You already know his better half, Acadia."

Ben winced inwardly but kept a smile on his face as the men all shook hands, and the mayor finished making introductions to the rest of the group. "Here's to the river walk project," the mayor said, raising his glass high.

"The river walk!" the men shouted in response before tossing back their drinks and then slamming the empty glasses onto the bar for refills.

As the evening wore on, Ben was introduced to nearly the entire group. Eventually, the hors d'oeuvres were cleared away and replaced with a full buffet of southern cuisine. Caterers scurried to and fro between the kitchen and the patio, balancing huge trays of food on their shoulders. Guests helped themselves and scattered about in small groups, both inside and out, taking advantage of seating wherever they could find it.

Ben hung at the bar for a while, wanting to get a better feel for Francois, the Realtor, and Alphonse, Acadia's husband. After all, he rationalized he'd probably be working closely with them in the months ahead. Francois was the older of the two and, it became clear, the more dominant. Running the family real estate enterprise was his main day-to-day focus, but he apparently was also a key confidant of his father, the mayor.

Francois was confident, almost cocky, but gracious toward Ben and seemed genuinely enthused about the project. He was interested to hear of Ben's modest football career at Boston College and casually let out the fact that back in the day, he had been the star tailback at Menard High, after which his football career had ended, and he'd gone on to Louisiana State to major in girls and business administration.

Alphonse was four years younger than Francois. They had no other siblings, and it was obvious Alphonse preferred to hang back in his brother's shadow and let him do most of the talking. While Francois entertained their guest, weaving stories of family exploits from the gridiron to business and politics, Alphonse imbibed a steady stream of Southern Comfort, hitting the bartender up frequently and listening quietly to his older brother's stories.

At one point, Ben turned to Alphonse to include him in the conversation, deeply curious to learn more about him.

"Alphonse, what is your role in the family enterprise? Will I be working with you as well?"

Alphonse regarded Ben evenly. His eyes were glassy, and his lips curled into a thin, crooked smile. "My role?" he said. "My role is to do whatever Pops and Big Brother here tell me to do. How would you categorize it, Big Brother? Community relations?"

Francois quickly jumped back in. "Yes, I would say community relations. Alphonse is much too modest, Mr. Johnson. I set a couple records running the ball. When Alphonse came along four years later, he was way better than me. Everyone knew it. Before the injury, he was the fastest, toughest, most elusive back you'd ever see. Everyone knew he had a ticket to D-1. He was the man in high school—best athlete, popular. Dated the prettiest girl. Wrecked his knee, and that was that. Worst injury I ever saw. Bent that leg straight back all the way to the hip, only the way it don't bend."

Alphonse banged his glass on the bar for another refill and then immediately threw down the next drink.

"Still married the prettiest girl in the parish. Ain't that right, Alphonse?"

Alphonse nodded. "That's right, Big Brother, and don't you forget it. I can still kick your ass, knee or no knee."

Francois gave his younger brother a friendly jab to the shoulder, to which Alphonse did not respond. Ben still wasn't sure exactly what Alphonse did, but he sensed that might be a good time to break off the conversation. He raised his glass in a last toast but took only a sip himself. "Nice meeting you, fellas. I look forward to working with you on the project. Excuse me. I'm going to grab some food." With that, he broke away and headed to the buffet. Behind him, Alphonse ordered another drink while his brother cautioned him that maybe he should slow down.

By ten o'clock, the crowd started to thin. The mayor was busy saying prolonged goodbyes, ever the politician. Alphonse was slumped in an oversized armchair in a corner of the living room. He looked as if he were struggling to stay awake. Except for their brief introduction and a glance from across the room, Ben had not been around Acadia all evening. He felt mildly disappointed, but after all, what had he expected?

Ben wasn't sure if young Billie Bob would be returning with the old Lincoln Town Car to give him a ride back to the hotel or if he should consider a taxi. He stepped out onto the patio for a breath of air, when he felt a presence at his elbow. It was Acadia.

"So you met the brothers, I see," she said in her silky, soft voice.

"Yes," Ben replied. "An interesting dynamic. Is there a bit of a sibling rivalry there?"

"You could say that. Francois is smart. He's also a go-getter. Like all the LaFleurs around here, he was popular in high school—a good athlete, good family. But Alphonse was the gifted one when it came to sports. He was the local high school hero. Then it all came apart on him. He never played again after that injury. He was never much of a student anyway. Playing sports was it for him. When he lost that, it seemed like he lost his spark. He just kind of drifted for a while, and after high school, he got into the family business."

"What exactly does he do for the family business?" Ben asked.

"It's hard to say. A little of this and a little of that. Mostly, I think, if something comes up in which the mayor and Francois don't want to get their hands dirty, they get Alphonse to do it."

"Things like what?"

"I don't always know exactly. I imagine things like collecting money or helping to persuade people to do some sort of deal they might not be so enthusiastic about. No one really talks about it."

"Is he a dangerous person to be around?"

"No, I don't think it's as bad as that. Maybe a little intimidation factor, but it's not like we're the Mafia around here. I guess you could say he's a kind of fixer, especially if it's something politically sensitive. He's a good father when he's sober. He'd never hurt me or the kids. I really don't think he'd seriously hurt anyone, unless they were a threat to the family."

Ben swallowed hard. "Remind me to never be a threat to the family."

Acadia laughed and gave him a subtle poke. "I don't think you have to worry about that."

"Francois said Alphonse married the prettiest girl in the parish. That would be you, right?"

"Well, that's very kind of Francois to characterize it that way, but yes, we went steady from eighth grade on. He was the most popular boy in the school. It seemed like a natural fit. The injury changed a lot of things, but it didn't change that. It was always just assumed that we'd marry after high school, and we did. That was twelve years ago. Where does the time go?"

"I don't know," Ben said. "It has a way of slipping by before we realize it. You mentioned kids. How many?"

"Two," Acadia replied. "A boy and a girl. Clement II is four, and Babette is seven."

Ben already knew she had kids, but still, it was hard to hear it. "That's wonderful," he said. "Sounds like the perfect family."

"No family is perfect, Mr. Johnson. I can assure you that."

Behind them, they heard a ruckus just inside the french doors. Francois was trying to raise his brother from the armchair, and Alphonse was protesting loudly. A cousin came over to assist, and one on each arm, they pulled Alphonse to his feet, where he stood unsteadily, trying to gain his bearings. His brother continued holding him by the arm. Alphonse tried to make a move to sit down again, but

Francois wouldn't let him. Most of the guests had already departed, with perhaps a dozen stragglers remaining.

The mayor came over to weigh in. "Phonse, if you can't hold your liquor, you're going to have to learn to slow down."

Alphonse tilted his head, looking at his father as if he were a curiosity of some sort. All at once, he pulled free of Francois's grip and broke into a jig, perhaps designed to demonstrate his sobriety. The dance went well for the first four or five steps, until he caught a toe and tumbled to the floor. Ben and Acadia watched from the french doors. Ben stole a sideways glance at Acadia, who had a passive look of resignation on her face, as if it weren't the first time she had seen such a performance and as if it were unlikely to be the last.

The mayor stepped in and took control, instructing Francois and his cousin to take Alphonse upstairs and put him to bed. The mayor approached Acadia and apologized. "I'm sorry, Miss Acadia. Will you be able to get home yourself, or would you like me to find someone to drive you? I don't think Phonse is going anywhere tonight."

"I'll be all right, Papa," Acadia replied, dropping the formal tone she'd used in the mayor's office when Ben first had met her as the ambassador of goodwill and reverting to family mode. "It's not like I'm not used to it. I can drive myself home."

"Okay," the mayor said with some regret. "I don't know what we're going to do with that boy. He's a good boy, but when the bottle gets ahold of him, he doesn't know how to put it down." There was a note of sadness to the mayor's voice. "You give those grandkids of mine a kiss good night when you get home, Acadia."

"I will, Papa. Don't you worry."

"All right, love, I'll send Phonse home tomorrow after he sleeps it off." The mayor gave his daughter-in- law a kiss and turned his attention to Ben, who took the opportunity to speak up.

"I really must be calling it a night as well. Can you have someone call me a cab?"

"Nonsense," Acadia said. "I can drop Mr. Johnson at his hotel. It's only a few minutes out of the way. It's no bother at all."

The mayor thought about that for a moment and then gave his approval. "Okay, if you don't mind. Just remember to give those grandkids that hug and kiss when you get home."

Ben protested mildly, but the decision had been made, and no one was going to allow him to wait around thirty minutes for a cab. The mayor apparently had assumed one of his sons or one of the cousins could give Ben a lift at the end of the night, but since Miss Acadia had volunteered, it was a fait accompli.

◆   ◆   ◆

Twenty minutes later, Acadia's Continental convertible pulled into the parking garage of the Bentley Hotel. Strangely, they had ridden in silence most of the way. Ben wasn't sure what to say about the way her husband had been hauled off to bed.

Acadia killed the engine and turned to face him. "Well, are you going to ask me up for a drink?"

"What about the kids?" he replied, uncharacteristically unsure of himself. "Don't you have to tuck them in?"

"I love my kids," Acadia said, "more than anything in the world, but they are already asleep. I hugged them and kissed them before I left the house. I'll hug them and kiss them when they wake up in the morning. The nanny is there to watch over them."

"What about your husband?" Ben asked uncomfortably.

"I don't want to talk about him right now. You saw him tonight. We'll talk about him some other time."

Without another word, she got out of the car and stood, waiting for Ben. Ben sat in the passenger seat for a moment, looking at her in the dim glow of the garage lighting. His heart was pounding, and a freight train was rushing through his head. His senses were all discombobulated. There was no doubt he wanted her, but he was scared. He knew right from wrong. This was wrong.

He got out of the car and walked to her. She took his hand, and they strolled silently through the garage and down two levels to the street below. Acadia discreetly dropped his hand before they hit the

24

open street. She lingered just inside the entrance to the garage. It was late, and there was no one else in sight.

"What room?" she whispered. Ben hesitated. "What room?" she repeated.

"Room 302," he replied robotically, as if he were listening to two other people.

"You go ahead. I'll meet you there in five minutes."

Ben turned and walked away, leaving her in the shadows of the doorway. He entered the lobby, which was largely empty except for the desk clerk and a couple sitting on a couch. To his left, he could hear laughter coming from the hotel bar. Even at his young age, with his business travels, he had entered all kinds of lobbies at all different hours without giving it a second thought. This time, he felt as though everyone knew his business, as though the couple and the desk clerk were staring at him.

He pushed the elevator button and gratefully escaped to the confines of the car when the doors slid closed. He fumbled for his key, exited the elevator on the third floor, and unlocked the door to room 302.

Once in the room, he sat on the bed, unsure what to do next. He realized he was trembling. What was he doing? This was a totally foreign experience. There were many things that could go wrong. What was he thinking? What would happen to the project if the mayor or his sons found out about this? What would his partners think? What would Alphonse do? After all, this was the Deep South. He was a black man with a married white woman. It was 1978. Things had changed somewhat since 1960, but the situation was still fraught with peril.

There was a knock on the door. Ben peered through the peephole and let Acadia in. He watched her carefully. What if all she really wanted was to have a drink and talk?

Acadia touched his shoulders gently with both hands and gave him a peck on the cheek, which he found confusing. "You go rest on the bed. I'm going to freshen up for a minute." She disappeared into the bathroom.

Ben felt as if he were standing in quicksand. What should he do? What had she meant by "freshen up"? Ben was always a gentleman. That was how he had been raised. Would she come back from the bathroom fully dressed? In that case, if he got naked, he would feel like a fool. On the other hand, if she came out naked and he was fully clothed, that would be bad too.

He decided to compromise. He removed his shirt and pants and carefully folded them over a chair but left on his T-shirt and boxer shorts. He climbed under the sheets and pulled them up to his chin. If she was offended in any way, he could apologize and get dressed without having caused too much trauma. If her intentions were clear, he could quickly make an adjustment the other way.

The door to the bathroom swung open. Her intentions were clear. She was an incredible sight, standing naked before him. She was more beautiful than he had even dared to imagine. Her skin and body were flawless; her face was like that of an angel. "What are you doing?" she asked with a note of surprise in her tone.

"Waiting for you," he replied softly.

She threw back the sheets in one motion, revealing his T-shirt and boxers. "Like that?" she said. "What did you intend to do?"

He smiled, slightly embarrassed. "I didn't want to offend you. I wasn't sure."

He was lying on his back. She climbed onto the bed and sat on top of him, pulling the T-shirt over his head. When his head popped through, her breasts were hanging inches from his face, her nipples protruding in anticipation. He leaned forward, sucking on one and then the other. She moaned softly, and he felt his manhood rapidly expanding beneath her. She rocked gently back and forth and then started kissing his chest. She took her time playing with the black curls with her delicate fingertips and kissing him all the way down.

She left his boxer shorts on, working all around the obvious protrusion that was stretching them tight. She kissed his thighs, moving from one to the other, and then gently rolled him onto his stomach as she pulled down his shorts. She continued kissing his back and butt. Ben was going crazy. It was the tenderest display of affection and foreplay he had ever known. She was appreciating every inch of his body, and he was in heaven.

As she had for him, he took his time, working his way down her softly contoured back, all the way to her butt, where he lingered a bit before moving on to the back side of her legs and calves. Her ample breasts hung freely over the bed, her nipples aching with extension. When neither of them could stand it any longer, he climbed atop her, pushing her back to the center of the bed. They consummated the love act in slow, rhythmic strokes as they kissed full on the mouth.

They made love six times that night. Never before had Ben experienced anything close to what happened. Their hunger for each other was impossible to satiate. In between sessions, they cuddled quietly in silence with their bodies intertwined and their fingers and lips exploring, waiting to recover until they were ready to go again.

When the morning sun began to slice through the crack where the window pull shades met, Acadia gave Ben one last kiss on the lips before retreating to the bathroom. She emerged ten minutes later, fully dressed, looking none the worse for wear. Neither of them had slept, but Acadia's natural energy radiated as brilliantly as ever, with not a hint of fatigue. Ben remained in the bed, naked under the sheets.

"Will you be all right?" he asked.

"Yes, I'll be fine. Alphonse won't be home until at least noon. He'll never know the difference. I'll be home before the kids are up. I'll have breakfast with them. The nanny might wonder where I was, but she's on my side, and she knows her place. She won't say anything. She won't even know what time I got in. I'll be home before she gets up as well."

Ben got up to give her a hug, still naked. Acadia turned her head slightly so as not to muss her lipstick. They embraced warmly, and Acadia turned to leave. "We'll talk later," she said.

"Yes," Ben replied. "We'll talk later." With that, she was gone.

Over the following weeks, they saw each other in passing a few times, mostly in and around city hall when Ben happened to be there while Acadia was meeting with someone in her role as ambassador of goodwill. There were always other people around. Once or twice, they also passed each other on the street. Acadia looked as beau...

as ever, but all they could do was exchange pleasantries and move on. The fire was still burning, but Ben worked hard to suppress the flames.

They lasted six weeks before the impasse was broken. Ben was lying on his bed in the suite at the Bentley Hotel, when he heard a knock on the door. It was Acadia. The mayor was at a conference in Baton Rouge, and Alphonse had accompanied him. They would be there for two nights. Acadia climbed onto the bed and held him for a long time.

"It's not my place to ruin your life," he said. "You've got two young children. If you're happy with Alphonse, we'll just keep what happened as a beautiful memory between the two of us."

"It's not Alphonse." Acadia sighed. "He has his own demons that I can't help him with. It's the whole entire picture—my family, his family, our children. There are expectations—and obligations. I'm trapped. Part of it is a sweet trap. I love my children. I can't ever leave them, hurt them, or embarrass them. Do you know what the culture is like down here? It's not just me who would suffer and be scandalized and ostracized. My children have their place. Francois doesn't have any kids. I don't think he and his wife can. My kids have a legacy, a birthright. There are three generations of political power, of empire building, of money and businesses, with tentacles everywhere. My children represent the next generation. I have no right to take that away from them."

"So you sacrifice yourself for them? Is that what you are saying?"

"Isn't that what mothers do?"

"I suppose," Ben replied.

They lapsed into silence once again. Acadia rested her head on his shoulder, and Ben put his arm around her. They lay watching TV. They stayed like that for almost two hours. Once again, she stayed until dawn, and once again, the time spent together was magical for ⁃h of them. They made love and talked and laughed, and when the ⁃me, Acadia went home to have breakfast with her children. ⁃ different when it came time to say goodbye. This ⁃l understanding. The construct of their ⁃n being together in the traditional sense, but it could not and would not prevent them from sharing a piece of their lives with each other—a special, intimate piece that would belong only to them.

They were at peace. Ben was no longer alone in the accommodation he'd made with himself. Acadia had joined him in that accommodation. They lived completely separate lives, but Ben drew two circles on a piece of hotel notepaper and placed each of their initials within a circle. The two circles overlapped in the middle, and Ben shaded in the common area with a pencil. Acadia smiled at him, took the paper, folded it, and tucked it away in her pocketbook. Ben repeated the process and put a second copy in his own wallet.

CHAPTER 5

Washington, DC: Present Day

Senator Richard Monroe rolled over and laid his head back on the pillow. The young woman next to him reached for her pocketbook on the nightstand and fished out a pack of cigarettes. She propped a pillow up against the headboard and lit up a smoke.

"I wish you wouldn't do that," the senator said resignedly. "It smells to high heaven."

"You say that every time, Dickie," she replied. "You're going to take a shower anyway, so what difference does it make?"

"It's not attractive. It turns me off."

The woman giggled. "Gee, you didn't seem to feel that way five minutes ago."

The senator waved his hand and swung his feet over the edge of the bed. "Ah, I can't win with you. I've gotta hit the head." He smiled to show he wasn't really angry but was just trying to make a point. The woman paid him no mind and continued to smoke while the senator went to the bathroom and closed the door.

It was not the woman's first time in the senator's Watergate apartment, and she doubted it would be her last. She knew how to please him, and a little cigarette smoke wasn't going to change that. She had known the senator for more than a year, and when in town, he was pretty much a regular customer. She reached for her cell phone and checked the time: one hour to go. *He'll probably try to rally for one last round.* She scrolled through her calendar to double-check the rest of her appointments for the day. Behind the bathroom door, she heard the toilet flush. She went to the Keurig machine across the room and stabbed her cigarette out in a coffee cup.

Daisy May was her professional name, and she tried to look the part—not in terms of cutoff jeans and a halter top but more along the lines of the way she wore her wild blonde hair up and the effect of her speech coming across like that of an innocent country girl. The customers loved that.

It wasn't that much of a stretch. At heart, Daisy May was a country girl. Endowed with certain natural talents, little education, and no small degree of ambition to climb out of poverty, she'd decided at a young age to use what God had given her. Men always had found her sexy and attractive. As she'd developed into a teenager, she'd discovered she had something of value, something men wanted. One thing had led to another, and now, at age thirty, she was living the good life as an elite professional escort in Washington, DC.

The service she worked for was top of the line and discreet. All her appointments were scheduled for her. Sometimes a single job could cover a few days, but more often, the average assignment was two or three hours. All the clients were powerful men and were well screened, and most were regulars.

She checked herself in the mirror, when suddenly, the senator's cell phone pinged. She glanced at the bathroom door. Curiosity got the better of her. Daisy May picked up the senator's phone. *It must be something, being important like he is*, she thought. *I wonder what it would be like. He probably gets calls and texts from generals, other senators, and maybe even the president.*

She read the text: "Thompkins is dead. SCOTUS operational. Meet ASAP. Usual. Final tgt authorization."

Someone is dead? Daisy May thought. *A relative of the senator or something?* Just as she was putting the senator's phone back on the nightstand, the bathroom door opened.

The senator saw her put the phone down. "Anything interesting?" he said.

Daisy May felt her face flush slightly. She flashed her sexiest smile. "No, Dickie, I was just coming back to bed when it pinged. It was just a natural reaction. It pinged, and I picked it up. I'm sorry."

Senator Monroe didn't seem angry. He picked up his phone and read the text. He immediately frowned.

"What is it, Dickie?" Daisy May said softly. "Did someone die or something? Is it someone you know?"

The senator stared at her but remained silent.

Daisy May smiled back innocently, not sure how to react.

Monroe retrieved his boxer shorts and trousers from a nearby chair and started to get dressed. Apparently, there would be no shower that day. "Daisy, be a love and see if you can find some news on the TV."

Daisy May pulled on her panties and blouse, clicked through a few channels, and found CNN. A banner scrolled across the bottom of the screen, proclaiming, "Breaking News: Supreme Court Justice Charles Thompkins Dead at 86." Pictures of Justice Thompkins in various scenes flashed on the screen as a newscaster intoned, "US Supreme Court Justice Charles Thompkins is dead of natural causes at age eighty-six. He passed away unexpectedly earlier this morning at his home in Bethesda, Maryland. Thompkins served on the court for parts of four decades and was a reliable vote for conservatives. Thompkins was first appointed to the court in—"

The senator reached over, took the control, and shut off the TV.

They both continued to dress in silence. It was obvious the lovemaking was through for the day. Senator Monroe seemed in a great hurry. Daisy May checked her makeup and hair one more time.

Monroe walked over, kissed the back of her head, and handed her ten crisp hundred-dollar bills. "I'm sorry, Daisy," he said. "I've got to go. You were wonderful, as usual. I'll see you again soon."

Daisy turned and kissed him on the cheek. "Thank you, Dickie. That was your friend, wasn't it? That guy on TV was the one in your text, right?"

Monroe didn't deny the obvious. "He's not actually my friend, just someone I know—someone important."

"All your friends are important, Dickie. That's one of the reasons I like you so much—that and the presents you give me." With that, Daisy May swung her pocketbook strap over her shoulder and left.

◆　◆　◆

Monroe's thoughts swirled. He was surprised Daisy May hadn't recognized the name of Supreme Court Justice Charles Thompkins. He felt a little relieved. What had he expected?

This was the opportunity he and the others had been waiting for. Thompkins, who'd been in ill health for years and was the oldest member of the court, was the key to the entire plan, the catalyst to put everything in motion. Monroe and his cohorts had been patient, banking on the fact that it would only be a matter of time. At one point, they even had considered the possibility of giving Justice Thompkins a nudge to help him transition from that life to the next, but they'd rejected the idea as too risky. Now their patience had paid off.

Two murders of Supreme Court justices in rapid succession would have created too much uncertainty. Such a circumstance might even have been viewed as part of a coup—which in fact, it would have been. Anything could have happened after that. It might have sparked a constitutional crisis or a national state of emergency. At the least, there would have been strong resistance and an uncertain result.

On the other hand, the natural death of an elderly justice followed by the unfortunate murder of another would be contentious but not so far out of the realm of possibility as to scream conspiracy. People were murdered every day in and around the DC area. It would be suspicious timing, and there would be much scrutiny and many calls to change the process, but ultimately, the process was in place for a reason and would be followed. After all, four presidents had been murdered in US history, and the rules of succession were always followed.

There would be no politically motivated assassination, merely an everyday occurrence of random violence that just happened to involve a young Supreme Court justice—an odd coincidence of timing but not something that would alter the protocols of the Constitution or spark a revolution. Of course, there would be loud protestations, much gnashing of teeth, conspiracy theories, and wild accusations. That was to be expected and could be dealt with. What mattered was the end result, and if the operation went as planned, the end result was preordained.

The country was more divided than ever, more so than Monroe could remember in his lifetime. There was a raging battle being fought for the soul of America. Congress continued to be split, with Republicans holding a slim margin in the Senate and the newly formed Democratic Socialist Party having taken solid control of the House. Monroe was smart enough to see the handwriting on the wall. More than half of young people in America favored socialism over capitalism. The more conservative traditionalists of the World War II generation and the baby boomers were dying off and being replaced at the ballot box by an entirely new demographic who had a different vision for the United States.

In addition to the shifting views of younger generations, twenty million undocumented workers would soon receive a path to citizenship and organize politically, creating an instant cushion and reliable voting block for the Democratic Socialists.

Now that conservatives had also lost the presidency, soon the recently completed walls on the southern border would be triumphantly torn down, much like the Berlin Wall in Germany. The North American continent was destined to follow the same course as Europe, an economic and political union with open borders. There would be a massive redistribution of wealth through the ballot box, with taxation and legislation used to create one huge middle class with little economic mobility.

In Monroe's view, the population would be cowed into economic and political acceptance. The education system and the media would reinforce how fortunate the citizenry were to live in a country with free health care for all, free education, free day care, food and medication stamps, and a government-provided base income that would continue all the way through retirement. Equality would be the mantra, and a willing population would fulfill their roles, many of them self-medicated on legalized drugs as they lived out their happy existences free of worry and void of ambition. That was the new American dream.

Of course, that would not be the fate of Senator Richard Monroe or any of the other members of his shadowy alliance. Throughout history, under every type of government and political system, there was always the ruling class. None of the rules applied to those elites. That was true from Communist China and Russia to the Third Reich of the Nazis and the kingdoms and dictatorships of the Middle East. It had been true from the earliest tribes and villages in ancient times, and it was true everywhere in the world in present day. Senator Richard Monroe was part of those ruling elite, and there was no way in hell he was ever going to give it up.

CHAPTER
6

Washington, DC

Monroe exited the Watergate and jumped into a cab at the head of the queue lined up outside the front entrance. Normally, he had his own driver, but when engaged in extracurricular activities at his Watergate apartment—usually hookers, card games, and drinking and occasionally meetings with leaders or operatives in his rapidly expanding dark network—he preferred to send the driver elsewhere as a decoy and cab it on his own.

Monroe instructed the cabbie to head to Arlington National Cemetery. His chief contact at the FBI was the one who'd called the meeting, and the topic was such that there was no point in taking any chances by meeting at a fixed location Monroe habitually frequented. The Watergate apartment was a well-kept secret, but a sudden and arbitrary stroll through Arlington Cemetery would provide a higher level of security.

Not everyone at the FBI—or the CIA or various other government intelligence agencies—was on board with Monroe's agenda, and he knew it could be a fatal mistake to underestimate their capabilities. As the cab wound its way through traffic, he felt a surge of adrenaline at the thought of what was about to go down. They were going to make history, and if they were successful, none but their innermost circle would ever know it.

Originally, they'd hatched the plot during an alcohol-fueled night of brainstorming. The previous president—a bombastic blowhard, in Monroe's estimate—had been in a unique historical position. He had been a one-term chief executive riding a wave of nationalistic populism to an upset Electoral College victory despite losing the popular vote by more than three million votes. Many saw his razor-thin margin of victory as the last gasp from a shrinking base of conservative traditionalists, fueled by disgruntled blue-collar Democrats throughout coal country, the rust belt, and the corn belt. With a few Bible thumpers thrown in, he had eked out the narrowest of victories. Notwithstanding his highly unlikely and improbable win, his base was shrinking every day, and the numbers working against him in the future had been insurmountable.

Most of what the last president had put in place could be readily undone now that the new Democratic Socialist Party was in control of the House and had won the presidency. Much could be accomplished through executive order, and all the data indicated that soon enough, the SocDems would take the Senate as well. When that happened, they would not squander the opportunity, as they had in the past when controlling both the executive branch and the Congress.

There were no longer any pretenses of civility or decorum between the two political parties. Once the Senate was taken, a new era would begin. The transition to a full-fledged socialist democracy would accelerate so quickly and comprehensively that there would be nothing conservatives could do to stop it.

Republican or Democrat, conservative or liberal, traditional or progressive, it was all secondary to Monroe. All his shadow government wanted was power, and they'd ally with anyone to attain it. He was confident he was on the right side of history.

As a US senator, he was already at the highest level of influence in the newly evolved Democratic Socialist Party. It had been a natural progression for him. He'd had to demonstrate through word and deed that he, a powerful middle-aged white man, was not part of the problem. Even though he had become the very definition of white privilege, he curried favor with the new electorate by embracing their causes. Like Bernie Sanders before him, he became a champion of young people and a clarion voice for minorities and immigrants, all of whom he regarded as the source of his own power.

The new America, the Green New Deal, open borders, free stuff— he was all in. If someone didn't agree with him, that person was a racist, sexist, or misogynist and part of the problem, not the solution. Privately, he had doubts as to how sustainable the new order would be, but he understood the momentum and recognized that the socialist wave had become an irresistible force. He figured it was better to ride the crest than drown in the undertow.

◆ ◆ ◆

The cab pulled into Arlington National Cemetery. There was only one major obstacle standing in the way of his master plan. It wasn't enough to control only two of three government branches. The obstacle was the Supreme Court. That day's meeting would finalize what was needed to control the third.

The recently departed Republican president had done his best to slow down the Democratic Socialist agenda. Through executive order, he had cut regulations, reduced the government's reach, and slowed illegal immigration. Legislatively, he'd pushed through lower taxes on businesses and generally promoted a procapitalism platform. The new administration could easily reverse all of that. What could not be easily reversed was the current makeup of the Supreme Court.

The one lasting legacy of the previous president was that through sheer luck of timing, he had had more opportunities to appoint new justices to the Supreme Court than any of his predecessors in recent history. When he first had taken office, the court had been perfectly balanced from an ideological standpoint. Four justices had leaned left, four justices had leaned right, and one had proven to be a swing vote, often siding with the liberals on matters of human rights while voting with conservatives on economic policy.

Supreme Court justices served lifetime appointments; most continued to a very old age, and many passed away as they continued to serve. In the long run, it was impossible to predict which party would be in control when a vacancy occurred in the distant future. Three vacancies had come up during the last presidential term. The swing-vote justice had retired, and two others had passed away from old age, one liberal and one conservative.

The Republican president had had the opportunity to appoint three justices during his tenure, all reliable conservatives. Within a single four-year term, he had been able to change the makeup of the court for decades to come. What had once been a balanced court was now slanted hard right, six to three in favor of conservatives.

The composition of the Supreme Court presented a significant problem for Monroe and his agenda. From his standpoint, the progressive train had left the station, and there would be no stopping it. He was on board that train, and the biggest threat to him going forward was the Supreme Court. An activist court was the only thing that could derail the train, and that was unacceptable.

Monroe made his way on foot to the Robert E. Lee Garden, where Harrington was waiting for him. Harrington casually strolled over to a nearby marker for one of the Civil War soldiers buried near Lee's old farmhouse. Monroe paused to look at a couple other graves and then appeared to randomly wander over near where Harrington was standing. They acted like strangers taking in a little history and enjoying a sunny DC afternoon.

Harrington spoke first, keeping his head down to minimize the chance of anyone overhearing and to guard against the remote possibility that they might be under surveillance and have a directional microphone pointed in their direction. "You were right to wait for Thompkins to go from natural causes," he said quietly. "It would have created one hell of an uproar if we'd killed both of them. Now no one can ever link the two deaths together. They can bitch all they want when we terminate Justice Sumner, but if we do it right, no one will ever be able to prove anything other than that he was an unlucky victim of random violence."

"That's the key," Monroe replied. "It has to appear to be random. There can be nothing that remotely suggests assassination or even a contract killing; I don't even want a gun involved. Make it a home invasion or a mugging or something like that."

"So are you giving me a go?" Harrington asked.

Monroe made eye contact with him and nodded. "Do you have the right personnel lined up for the job?"

This time, Harrington nodded in assent.

"Good," Monroe said. "I don't want to know any details. I want plausible deniability up and down the chain. All the president needs to know is that when the time comes, he has two openings to fill. He never has to know the second opening was anything more than shit luck. Once he fills those vacancies, the court will no longer be an impediment. We will control two and a half branches of government. The Senate won't be far behind. When we get the Senate, we'll have the entire government, all three branches. That is the ultimate mission. Once we have that, we will never relinquish them again. Our position will be unassailable. We will have lifetime control."

"It will be done," Harrington said.

"What is the time frame?" Monroe asked.

"I'm not sure. Four to six weeks, I am thinking. You will know when you see it in the news."

"Good." Monroe hesitated. "There may be another problem."

"What?"

"There's a woman. She was in my apartment at the Watergate. She saw your text."

"How could you let that happen? Who is she?"

"She's an escort, Frank. I was in the other room when you texted. She picked up the phone and read the text. I caught her in the act."

"Did she know what she was reading?"

"I don't know. I don't think so, but we can't take a chance. There can be no loose ends."

"I understand. I'll take care of it. What is her name?"

"Her professional name is Daisy May. I don't know her real name. She works for the Premiere Escort Service. You can find her online."

"Okay, we'll find her. Don't bother to book any more appointments with Daisy May," Harrington said.

CHAPTER 7

Boston, Massachusetts

Alone in the back of the cab, Ben Johnson removed the worn forty-year-old piece of paper from his wallet. He tenderly unfolded it and laid it on his thigh. His finger gently caressed the shaded area. Forty years of separate lives and shared love. His expression hardened. No matter what it took, he would find out who had hurt his Acadia. He owed her that.

The driver dropped Ben right in front of 161 Berkley Street, at the entrance to Grille 23. As was his habit, Ben was five minutes early for his noon lunch meeting. In the twenty-four hours since he'd received the devastating news about Acadia, his emotions had run the gamut. Now he was determined to find out what really had happened, and there was only one person he trusted enough to ask for that kind of help.

The maître d' escorted Ben to his usual table in a secluded corner of the restaurant. It was no surprise to Ben that Dimase Augustin was already there, seated at the table, waiting patiently. Punctuality was one of the many qualities Ben admired about Dimase.

Dimase had emigrated with his parents from Haiti when he was ten years old. In his professional life, after six years spent with US Army Special Forces, Dimase had risen through the ranks at Cambridge PD, ultimately serving as the head of homicide investigations for several years. Ben admired the man's passion, sharp mind, and unparalleled work ethic, attributes they had in common, which served to strengthen the bond between them. Recently, Dimase had retired from the Cambridge PD and set up shop with Bill Larson, a forensic psychologist and former detective with the FBI. According to their website, Augustin and Larson Confidential LLC specialized in sensitive investigations, security consulting, corporate counterespionage, and government contracting.

Dimase rose to greet him, and the two embraced warmly. Dimase was one of the few who knew about Ben and Acadia.

"What is it, my friend?" Dimase asked. "You look upset. Something has happened. What?"

Ben brought Dimase up to speed on the phone call from Amandine and the sequence of events leading to Acadia currently being in a coma. "For obvious reasons, I can't be with her right now. I need to know what happened. Who did this to her, and why? I need you to go down there. I need you to make sure she is safe and getting the best care, and I need to know who is responsible. Will you do this for me?"

Dimase reached across the table and took his friend's hand in his own. "You know I will do this for you. I promise you we will get to the bottom of it. I will leave tomorrow."

◆　◆　◆

Alexandria, Louisiana

Twenty-four hours later, Dimase Augustin was ensconced in a suite at the Bentley Hotel, the same hotel where, unbeknownst to him, Ben and Acadia had had their first tryst after the party at the mayor's house many years ago. He'd already paid a courtesy visit to the sheriff to advise the locals of his presence and the purpose of his visit.

Despite Dimase's background as a former homicide detective, the sheriff had given him a cool reception. Of course, Dimase could not disclose that he was in Alexandria at the behest of Ben Johnson. Client confidentiality aside, there was no plausible reason Ben would send down a private detective to investigate a local home invasion. That information would have raised all kinds of red flags with the sheriff and no doubt would have made its way back to the LaFleur family in no time.

Ben and Acadia had kept their secret that long, and there was no reason to make Acadia's family aware of it now. Ben had given Dimase strict instructions that Acadia's reputation was not to be compromised in any way, particularly with her husband and children, especially when she lay helpless in a coma. No purpose would have been served at that point in her life by opening that door and putting it right in their faces that Acadia's life was not perfect and that she was a real woman who lived, loved, lusted, and hurt like everyone else.

Instead, Dimase had concocted a story about a series of home invasions in the greater Boston area with a possible tie to Louisiana. It was weak but better than nothing. He'd told the sheriff there were three cases with a similar MO, in which a baseball bat had been used to attack a wealthy homeowner. A letter had been found in a desk drawer at the scene of the last attack. It was an attempt to extort money from the victim in return for the suppression of some unknown information. The letter had been postmarked from Alexandria, Louisiana, two weeks ago.

Dimase had explained that his partner, Bill Larson, had used his forensic expertise to search for similar home-invasion attacks in the Alexandria area, and when the sheriff's police report had gone into the data system, they'd had a hit. At that point, they'd connected their case to the sheriff's case because of the extortion letter; the two similar attacks had occurred hundreds of miles apart, but the postmark indicated that the Boston perpetrator could have been in Alexandria at the time Ms. LaFleur was attacked. "That's all we have," he had told the sheriff. "That's why I'm here."

Without saying so, the sheriff had made it clear he didn't like outsiders meddling in his investigation and especially did not like private citizens getting involved. Nonetheless, the fabrication served its purpose and provided cover for why Dimase was in Alexandria and why he would be poking around. There was nothing the sheriff could do to stop him; he just was not going to go out of his way to help Dimase out. The sheriff had ended the conversation with an admonition for Dimase to let him know if he uncovered anything of significance.

Later that afternoon, Dimase decided to stop by the hospital where Acadia was being treated. He was not allowed to visit her room since he was not a family member or a proper authority with a warrant. Instead, he hung out in the hospital lounge, hoping to catch Acadia's husband or children on their way in or out. Family cooperation would make everything easier.

Eventually, his patience paid off. As the dinner hour approached, he saw Acadia's husband, Alphonse, and her two children, Clement II and Babette, walking down the corridor toward him. He quickly jumped to his feet and introduced himself, producing his identification as a PI. "I'm only here to help if I can," Dimase said. "I know the local police are working on this, but if there is a connection to my case in Boston and I can help find out who did this to your mom and your wife, would you not want me to do that? Please, may we have a seat just for a moment?"

Dimase guided them to a corner of the lounge, where they could have some privacy. He could see that the eyes of both of Acadia's adult children were red from crying. Her husband, Alphonse, looked distraught as well but seemed more reticent to sit down.

"We have reason to believe that someone who either lives in or visits the Alexandria area may be trying to extort money from wealthy victims." Dimase went on to explain the connection to his make-believe case in Boston, saying that the MO was similar and that an extortion letter from Alexandria, postmarked within the past two weeks, had been found hidden away in a desk drawer in the latest victim's home. "Are you aware of any attempt to extort money from your family, either from Miss Acadia or from any of you?"

They all shook their heads, and Dimase continued. "The local authorities are not really pursuing the extortion angle. May I have your permission to interview people connected to your home and perhaps connected to your family as well? I would be discreet and respectful. I have many years of experience in these matters."

Dimase went on to fill them in on his background as former chief homicide detective for the city of Cambridge, Massachusetts, and his current partnership with Bill Larson. "With all due respect to the sheriff and his department, Bill and I have expertise and background they simply don't have. Our only objective is to help find out who is responsible for these heinous crimes. I would like to start by interviewing servants, workers on your property, and anyone else who might have come in contact with Miss Acadia. Will you let me do this for you?"

Dimase was convincing. Alphonse seemed hesitant, perhaps as a natural by-product of his murky family role as fixer and facilitator. Clement II had no such reservations and said, "Mr. Augustin, as mayor of this city, I can assure you that if you can help us find out who did this to my mother, you will have the full resources and cooperation of my people. I want this son of a bitch, and I don't really give a shit whether you, Sheriff Roy, or one of us gets him. You tell me what you need, and I'll make sure you get it."

They all stood, and Clement II solemnly shook Dimase's hand. Alphonse and Babette remained quiet and reserved.

"You get that son of a bitch," Clement II said again for emphasis. With that, the family members turned and walked away.

Dimase smiled to himself despite the gravity of the situation. He had been in Alexandria for less than a day and now had unfettered permission to launch a full-scale private investigation.

CHAPTER
8

Three days later, the investigation had turned up nothing.

Dimase had been in that position many times before, and all he could do was keep looking and wait it out. More times than not, some new fact or circumstance came to light, serving as the catalyst to break the impasse and open up new avenues to pursue. In his line of work, patience was not only a virtue; it was a necessity.

Since Dimase's conversation with Mayor Clement II and the mayor's expression of support for Dimase's investigation, Sheriff Roy had become notably more cooperative. At Dimase's urging, the authorities checked all entrances to LaFleur House, looking for latent fingerprints that did not match family members or workers. A partial print was found on a panel of the back door. It was not a match for anyone in the control group of people frequenting the house, but neither was it in any of the databases they ran it through.

Dimase also considered the possibility of DNA and fiber evidence. He asked the family for permission to cordon off the stairs and the area of attack at the top landing until he could complete a more minute examination. Although Acadia had now been in a coma for a few days, he also asked if he could visit her in the hospital. He assumed she would be heavily bandaged, and there would be no way to examine her wounds, but he wanted to see her in person and get a feel for her condition.

Mayor Clement II agreed to meet and escort Dimase to his mother's room later that afternoon. At two o'clock, Dimase was waiting in the hospital lounge, when the mayor approached. "Have you been able to find anything yet?" the mayor asked.

"Nothing substantive, but we have a long way to go, Mr. Mayor. These things take time. We are covering all the bases. When we least expect it, some fact will reveal itself, and the picture will become more clear. What that might be and when we will see it I do not know."

The mayor guided Dimase down the hall and into his mother's room.

Acadia did not look like the beautiful woman Dimase remembered from their prior meetings. The back and top of her head were fully encased in bandages, and her eyes, though closed, were black and blue, shrouded in bruises and pockets of pooled blood. The visible portion of her face was severely swollen, and a respirator fed oxygen through a tube inserted in her throat. An IV tree stood next to the bed, along with a heart monitor. Tangles of wires and tubing either attached to her arm or wound under the blankets. Acadia's chest rose and fell almost imperceptibly to the rhythm of the breathing machine. One leg was elevated and in a cast from ankle to thigh. One arm was also in a cast and immobilized in a sling on her chest.

The mayor kissed his mother on the forehead and pulled up a chair to be near her side. Dimase gently took her hand and bent close to examine it. If he had been at the scene of her attack when she first had been discovered, one of the first things he would have done was check under her fingernails for skin, blood, or any indication she had fought back and scratched her attacker before he was able to deliver the blow that sent her down the stairs.

It was perhaps unlikely she would have had time to get a hand on him, particularly given the apparent angle of attack and the likelihood that the attacker had surprised her from behind. Nonetheless, Dimase ran an imaginary video replay through his head, a technique he used frequently to try to reconstruct a crime scene. He could picture the possibility that Acadia might have been facing her attacker, possibly resisting, before being shoved and spun toward the top of the stairs, where the blow was then delivered from behind.

Dimase carefully and delicately held her fingertips one by one. Too much time had gone by for any useful material to be present under her fingernails. She had been sponge-bathed several times in the past few days. There was one item of interest. Dimase remembered her beautifully manicured fingernails on the two occasions they had met in Boston. Now, in the hospital, the subtle pink polish on her nails was starting to chip and fade. On the index finger of her right hand, the nail was raggedly broken off in an uneven pattern near the base. *Where is that broken nail?* Dimase wondered.

Dimase thanked the mayor and left him sitting with his mother. Outside the hospital, he punched Sheriff Roy's number on his cell phone. "Sheriff, Dimase Augustin here. Tell me—did anyone in your department vacuum the area at the top of the stairs or try to collect any fiber or other evidence?"

"No. Remember, when the first responders showed up, they just thought it was a terrible accident and that she fell down the stairs. Their only priority was to stabilize Miss Acadia and get her to the hospital. It was only later that we looked at it as a crime scene and went back to take some pictures after the docs gave us the heads-up on the nature of her injuries."

"I see," Dimase replied. "I thought that might have been the case, but I just wanted to make sure."

"Why do you ask?"

"Nothing in particular," Dimase said. "I might just take a look around to see if anything's there. It's a long shot. There may be some disturbance from first responders and also from your guys, but most of their activity would have been centered on Acadia, where she lay at the bottom of the stairs. Maybe I'll get lucky and find something."

Dimase retrieved his rental Ford Escort from the hospital parking lot and set out for the LaFleur residence. He parked out front, rang the doorbell, and was greeted by the butler.

Dimase took off his shoes and left them at the bottom of the stairs. He pulled a magnifying glass from his pocket and carefully crept up the stairs in his stocking feet. On the landing at the top, he got down on his hands and knees and started to examine the carpet inch by inch. He covered the entire area without result, slowly expanding the search radius beyond the immediate landing. He was pretty much at the limit of what he thought would be a reasonable search zone, when he found it. There, beyond the carpet, on the hardwood between railing spindles, was the missing piece of Miss Acadia's fingernail.

Dimase removed tweezers and a small baggie from his pocket. Using the tweezers, he turned the nail over. It was pink on one side. Underneath, he saw a dark stain near the tip end of the nail and specks of dirt or some other material. He placed the partial nail in the small plastic bag and tucked it in the breast pocket of his shirt. Maybe this was the break he had been waiting for. It was time to call Ben Johnson.

CHAPTER
9

Boston, Massachusetts

Ben Johnson was sitting in the executive lounge at Boston's Logan Airport, when he felt the vibration of his cell phone in his pocket. He looked at the caller ID and immediately picked up when he saw Dimase Augustin's name. "Good afternoon, my friend. How are you making out down there?" Ben asked.

Dimase launched into a lengthy explanation, bringing Ben up to speed on how he'd been able to get Mayor Clement II's permission to essentially launch a full-scale private investigation.

"Excellent," Ben responded. "I knew I could count on you to stir things up and move them forward. I don't trust the locals. They may or may not be well intended, but either way, they can't possibly have the experience and expertise that you and Bill Larson have. Are they cooperating with you?"

"Yes," Dimase said. "Once the mayor endorsed my investigation, they didn't have much choice. The sheriff is a guy named Roy—last name Roy. You ever hear of him?"

"No," Ben replied. "I haven't been involved in any of the operations of our Alexandria properties for many years. Once we finished the river walk development, I pretty much stayed away from Alexandria, for reasons I'm sure you can appreciate. I kept a low profile with the LaFleurs. When Acadia and I spent time together, it was far away from Alexandria. Is Sheriff Roy related to the LaFleurs in any way?"

"Not that I know of," Dimase said. "It's certainly possible, but either way, he wouldn't be the sheriff if he wasn't beholden to them somehow."

"I suppose that's true," Ben said. "Does he know what he's doing?"

"I think becoming sheriff is an elected position down here, which makes it more political than professional. Let's just say it's a good thing you sent me down here to back things up. I may have come up with something that can help us. The first responders thought they were responding to an accident, not a crime, and thus, they didn't treat it like a crime scene. They trampled all over the carpet and didn't preserve the scene when they were attending to Miss Acadia. It was only later, when the doctors at the hospital saw the nature of the head wound and notified the sheriff, that they realized a crime had been committed. He sent his men back to take some pictures, but beyond that, they didn't do much."

"So what have you come up with?" Ben asked hopefully.

"Two or three things," Dimase replied. "Some may be more helpful than others. We will have to see. I found a partial fingerprint on the back door. We ran it through all the databases we have access to and did not get a match. It can be tough with only a partial. The print may be more helpful if we have a suspect in the future and want to place that person at the LaFleur residence."

"What else?" Ben asked.

"I went to the hospital to visit Miss Acadia."

Ben drew in his breath. "How did she look?" he asked anxiously. "Do you think she has a chance?"

"I can't lie to you, Ben. She's in rough shape. I wish I could tell you she'll be okay, but at this point, that is in God's hands. I did find something, though. The nail on her right index finger was sharply broken off at the base. It did not look like something that would happen in her normal activities. We both know how meticulous Miss Acadia is about maintaining her nails. I concluded there was a good possibility she may have broken the nail while resisting her attacker."

"What does that mean? How does it help us?" Ben asked.

"For one thing, it means she may have been facing her attacker at some point. If that is the case, she may actually know who it is or be able to later identify that person from a photo or in a lineup."

"You're assuming she'll come out of the coma for that to happen. I pray to God you are right," Ben said.

Dimase continued. "It also means we could get some DNA if she scratched him or made contact in some way. I went back to the scene, and I went over every inch of the stairs and landing. I found the missing piece of her nail by the railing, near the second-floor landing. To the naked eye, it appears as though there is blood and possibly skin on the underside. I've bagged it and have it with me now, and then I called you right away."

Ben thanked his friend profusely for his efforts and complimented him on his abilities. "What's the next step?"

"We need to discuss that," Dimase said. "Technically, I should turn the nail over to the sheriff, and it would be up to him what to do with it. I am reluctant to do that. First, there is the issue of competence. I don't know that I trust them not to taint the evidence and blow the whole thing. After all, they didn't even check for fiber or DNA in the first place. I doubt they have much experience in handling this type of thing. That's my main concern. I suppose there's also a remote possibility of corruption—probably not the sheriff himself but possibly someone under his command. If the crime was committed by a local—and we don't have a motive yet—there's no guarantee that some level of corruption couldn't extend into the sheriff's department. My gut tells me we should keep this evidence to ourselves for now. I can ship it off to Bill Larson, and he can use his contacts at the FBI lab to take a look at it."

"Good call," Ben said. "I'm with you on that. How long will it take for the FBI to come up with something?"

"It's hard to say, Ben. They may never come up with anything if we don't have something to match it against. They can do some level of analysis, and if there is enough material on the nail, they can create a DNA profile. It's not like fingerprints, for which we have huge databases on record. They can compare the profile to what DNA databases exist. Even at the FBI, it could take a while for them to develop the DNA profile and run it through any existing databases."

"Okay, I understand," Ben said, mildly disappointed.

"Keep your chin up," Dimase said. "I'll keep you informed."

Ben thanked his friend again and ended the call. As much as he wanted answers right away, Dimase had made remarkable progress in the short time he'd been in Alexandria. Ben noted the time: five minutes till boarding for his late-afternoon flight to Washington, DC. He gathered up the documents he'd been reading before taking Dimase's call and stuffed them back into his soft leather briefcase before heading to the gate.

As hard as it was with Acadia lying in a coma, he had to focus on the task at hand. Tomorrow was a big day. The winds of change were blowing across the country. Fischer, Forbes, and Johnson had always tried to maintain political neutrality, keeping up relations on both sides of the aisle. As the country leaned further and further left and the partisan divide became more rancorous by the day, walking that tightrope had become increasingly difficult. In the world of commerce, there would clearly be winners and losers. Ben's job was to ensure that Fischer, Forbes, and Johnson came out on the winning side. He had to stay ahead of the curve.

For decades, the country had put off any major federal investment in what was now a crumbling national infrastructure. All across America, roads and bridges were in desperate need of upgrade and repair, unable to keep up with the burgeoning population. Utilities, including cable and internet, needed substantial technological improvement and massive network expansion as well as to be submerged below ground.

Fischer, Forbes, and Johnson had been built through property development, management, and ownership. Now, as Ben looked to the future, he saw that a strategic shift was required. The greatest federal expenditure in history was about to begin, a massive twenty-year deployment of money and resources devoted to a complete overhaul of the national infrastructure. Ben realized the future of Fischer, Forbes, and Johnson might depend on his ability to positon the company in the middle of the infrastructure initiative. The future was at ground level and below. The customer would be the federal government.

The meeting the next day in DC was his launch. He had to have his fastball tomorrow. Senator Richard Monroe of Illinois was the new chairman of the powerful Senate Finance Committee. Ben knew the man but not well. That was about to change.

Ben had requested the lunch meeting through Monroe's staff, and the senator had been happy to oblige. Monroe was an emerging player. His hands would be on the purse strings of the entire infrastructure program. If Fischer, Forbes, and Johnson were to survive and thrive in the years ahead, it was incumbent upon Ben to change the perception of the company. That transformation would begin tomorrow at lunch with Senator Richard Monroe of Illinois.

CHAPTER
10

Alexandria, Louisiana

Dimase shipped the broken fingernail off to his partner, Bill Larson. One of the advantages of going private with Bill, in addition to his partner's keen mind and superb investigative skills, was Bill's relationship with the FBI. As a former FBI forensic psychologist and, prior to that, head of homicide investigations for the Massachusetts State Police, Larson had more contacts than pretty much anyone, and their firm had a stellar reputation. That gave them a solid network of sources. Both the feds and the state authorities consulted with them regularly.

Despite the strong support system based back in Boston, Dimase was pretty much on his own in Alexandria. Larson got the ball rolling on the DNA analysis of the fingernail, but at best, assuming there was material they could work with, it would takes days to develop a profile, with no assurance they would find any kind of a match in known databases.

Dimase pondered what he should do next. All the staff, servants, and family members he'd interviewed had reasonable alibis, and none had any apparent motive. Investigators always had to consider family members in a case like this one. Dimase had had some interaction with the immediate family, but on the face of it, there didn't seem to be anything there either. Acadia's husband, Alphonse, had clearly been in Washington, DC, at the time of the attack. Her son, Mayor Clement II, had been in city hall, surrounded throughout the day by a variety of municipal employees and constituents as he conducted business as usual. Her daughter, Babette, had first heard the news when she was doing volunteer work at her children's school.

The family seemed to be in the clear, but so did everyone else. It was a baffling case. Robbery did not appear to be a motive. No note or prior correspondence demanding money had been found. An extortion plot gone wrong did not seem to be a viable motive. The LaFleur children, by all accounts, loved their mother and lived a comfortable, affluent lifestyle. Inheritance did not seem to be a motive. Neither was sexual assault.

Dimase thought about the house, which was not somewhere one went on a casual stroll. There were no vagrants in the area, so if the attacker hadn't been an arbitrary person passing through and there was no obvious motive, that left only one alternative: a contract hit.

Then Dimase saw a third possibility. If it hadn't been a break-in by a homeless vagabond or a politically motivated hit job, could it have been for love? That idea brought him back to Alphonse. Was it possible Alphonse had known about Acadia and Ben Johnson for all those years? Or maybe he only recently had found out. Could he have hired someone to do the job out of pride, jealousy, or revenge? When he looked at it in that light, Alphonse became as strong a suspect as anyone.

Dimase had been sitting at the desk in his hotel room, manipulating an unlit cigarette between his fingers as he ran different scenarios through his mind and sketched out notes on a small pad. First things first, he decided. It was time to start narrowing down the possibilities. He picked up his phone and made arrangements to meet with the sheriff.

An hour later, he was sitting across from Sheriff Roy, reviewing his thought process from earlier in the day.

"So you actually think it might be a homeless person?" the sheriff asked. "We don't get much of that around here. It's not like a big city."

"Actually, Sheriff, I really don't think that's it. I just want to rule it out. Did your boys pick up anyone like that in the days around the attack? Are there any hippies living in the woods or any local drunks who get lost from time to time?"

"No, I don't think so," the sheriff replied. "I mean, we have a few habitual drunks, like anyplace else, but I've never known any of them to wander out of town in that direction. I'll double-check the arrest records. I don't think we picked up anyone like what you're describing."

"Okay, I had to ask. If you see anything that should point us in that direction, will you let me know?"

"Of course," the sheriff replied. "So you think it was a hit?" His eyes were open wide.

"I don't know," Dimase said, "but right now, it fits better than any other explanation. Wouldn't you agree?"

"I suppose so," the sheriff said, "but who would order such a thing? And why?"

Dimase decided to continue to play his cards close to the vest. He still hadn't mentioned anything to the sheriff about the partial nail he'd recovered. He also didn't want to say anything about Alphonse being on his list of possibilities for arranging a hit on Acadia. Sharing that information with the sheriff would probably have been a fast track to getting thrown off the case if the sheriff leaked word back to Alphonse or any of the LaFleurs. "I don't know, but that's what we have to find out," Dimase said, standing and shaking the sheriff's hand.

Just then, one of the sheriff's deputies stuck his head in the door. "Sheriff, I've got the sheriff from Beauregard Parish on the line. You two are both going to want to hear about this."

Dimase and Sheriff Roy looked at each other, and Dimase sat back down.

"Put him through," the sheriff said.

"Who are they?" Dimase asked.

"Two parishes over, about sixty miles from here," Sheriff Roy replied. He picked up the phone on his desk. "Roy here. Yes. Yes, I see.

No shit. Jesus H. Christ, you have to be shitting me. You think there's a connection? All right, send me what you've got, and I'll send you our file. Yeah, check it out, and let's talk. Okay, right. Thanks."

Dimase looked at Sheriff Roy expectantly. "What's going on?"

"You're not going to believe it," Roy replied. "We've got a murder that might be connected to Miss Acadia."

Now it was Dimase's turn to look wide-eyed. "How so?" he asked.

"Home invasion. Single woman home alone. Guess what he killed her with? A baseball bat is what it looks like. Beat her to death."

"Oh shit!" Dimase exclaimed.

"That's nothing," Roy said. "Guess what her name was?"

"No clue," Dimase said.

"Acadia LaFleur."

CHAPTER 11

Dimase realized there was no possible way the second attack could be a coincidence. There had to be a connection.

Dimase turned to the sheriff. "How many Acadia LaFleurs are out there?"

Sheriff Roy stroked a few keys and leaned back in his chair so Dimase could see the screen. "There's a lot more of them than I would have thought!" the sheriff exclaimed. "LaFleur is a pretty common Cajun name, and there're also French Canadians throughout the United States with the surname LaFleur. Says here Acadia is actually a region in Canada, around what we now think of as Nova Scotia and New Brunswick, that was originally populated by Native Indians and French settlers. There was some intermingling of those two groups. Eventually, after a bunch of wars, the English took over, and a lot of what we now call Cajuns migrated to the United States, many of them winding up right here in Louisiana. Says Acadia is one of the most common female Cajun names, after the region in Canada where they all came from. According to this, guess how many Acadia LaFleurs there are in the US?"

"No idea," Dimase said, straining to read what was on the screen as the sheriff scrolled rapidly back and forth.

"Fourteen hundred or so in the whole country and over four

hundred right here in Louisiana. It's the Cajun equivalent of the name Jane Smith or Sue Jones, for cryin' out loud. There's tons of them."

"When was the last time you had a victim of any sort by that name?" Dimase asked.

The sheriff turned to face him. "Can't recall that we ever have," he said.

"So what do you think the odds are that we have two victims with the same MO and the same name within two weeks?"

"Not very high, I'd say. What the hell do you think is going on?" the sheriff asked.

"I don't know," Dimase replied, "but it seems obvious that we're probably looking at the same perp. It has to be the same guy. It's too much of a coincidence to be anything else."

"Do you think we should put some kind of warning out to people named Acadia LaFleur? Maybe we have some kind of crazed serial killer working his way through a telephone directory or census listing."

"That's possible, I suppose," Dimase said, "but I don't think that's it. Nonetheless, you probably should put out a communication to all the sheriffs' departments and the Louisiana State Police, alerting them and advising them to contact any Acadia LaFleur within their jurisdiction."

"I can do that," the sheriff said. "What are you going to do?"

"How would you feel about deputizing me and allowing me to go down to Beauregard Parish to check things out?"

The sheriff just stared at him.

"All due respect, Sheriff, your men are not trained for this type of investigation. I am. It's outside your jurisdiction anyway. Let me be your liaison between the two cases. If I can help us make progress, it will only make you look better. I'll report straight back to you on anything I discover down there." Dimase was intentionally specific in mentioning "down there." He still didn't want to share with the sheriff the discovery of the partial fingernail he had shipped off for DNA analysis.

The sheriff thought about Dimase's offer for a moment. Then he shrugged and accepted. "All right, consider yourself deputized, but I want to know what the hell is going on down there and how it relates to what we have going on back up here. All hell is going to break loose when word of this gets out. The mayor is going to be all over my ass. Everyone's going to want answers, and I haven't got any."

Dimase stood. "Let them know I'm coming. Try to smooth the way for them to be cooperative. I'll see what I can do."

◆　◆　◆

The next morning, Dimase got an early start on the drive to Deridder, the seat of Beauregard Parish, which was about a seventy-mile ride. Sheriff Roy had called ahead and made a ten o'clock appointment for him with Sheriff DeWitt.

Beauregard was a sprawling parish of almost twelve hundred square miles, located southwest of Alexandria, with a population of about thirty-six thousand people, a third of whom were clustered in and around Deridder. The balance of the populace was more rural, with significant pockets of poverty. The murder of the other Acadia LaFleur had taken place in Sugartown, a small unincorporated community about seventeen miles east of Deridder that was little more than a crossroads on the map.

Dimase's meeting was at the sheriff's office in Deridder, but he hoped at some point they would allow him to visit the house in Sugartown where the murder had taken place.

Sheriff DeWitt was ready and waiting. He was a rotund man in his late fifties, with sleepy eyes that appeared to be half closed. He motioned for Dimase to take a seat. "Good mawnin', Detective Augustin," he drawled. "My counterpart in Alexandria says you are just the man to help us out. Is that so?"

The man exuded low energy. Dimase hoped that would work to his advantage.

"I'm here to help if I can," Dimase replied. "What have we got?"

DeWitt slid a thick folder across the desk. "This heah is for you. I had a copy made for y'all. We don't get much of this type of thing around heah. Every few years, we might git a killin'. Usually there ain't nuthin' to solve—you know, domestic violence—some guy beats up his ole lady, and it gits out of hand—or a bar fight or sumpin' like that. The one that done it is right there. There ain't no mystery. We arrest 'em, they plead out, and whatever happens happens."

"What do you think happened here?" Dimase asked.

"Well, we ain't got no suspects. The victim ain't even lived in these parts for quite a while. She grew up heah, but she took off a few years ago—don't know where to. Her ma lives out by the melon fields in an old place off Route 112. Nuthin' more than a glorified shack, really. The ma says her daughter just showed up outta the blue 'bout two weeks ago. Said she seemed scared 'bout sumpin' but wouldn't say what."

"Where was her mother at the time of the attack?"

"The ma don't have a car," the sheriff replied. "She's on welfare, and her health ain't so good. Every Thursday night, she goes to bingo at the church. The church got an old van, and they send a guy out to pick people up that cain't get there on their own—you know, kinda an outreach program to help old folks and such and them that live alone."

"How did the daughter get here? Did she have a car?"

"No, the ma says she came by bus and walked from the drop-off out on 112."

Dimase thought that was odd, but he didn't say anything. "So what happened?"

"The van dropped the ma back home 'bout nine thirty. When she went inside, she found her daughter. It was sumthin' awful. Whoever done it beat the shit outta her—blood and brains everywhere. It was a real mess. Such a pretty girl from the pictures I seen and as I remember her from years ago. You couldn't recognize her. It's almost like someone was really angry 'bout sumthin'—just left her a pulp." He nodded toward the folder. "There. Look for yourself."

Dimase opened the folder and flipped through a series of about twenty photos. The sheriff wasn't exaggerating. "What's the mother say? She have any idea who might have done this?"

"I talked to her some. She's pretty shook up. She couldn't tell us much, but we should probably talk to her again when she done calmed down. Pretty much all she could do when I talked to her was sobbin' and cryin'. There was no way she could stay out there, so we put her up in a roomin' house here in town, near the church. We roped off the scene, took them pictures, and called the coroner and the state police. I think they took their own pictures and some blood and tissue and such and removed the body to the morgue at the hospital. I knew about the Acadia LaFleur attack up in Alexandria 'cause everyone know about the congressman and that whole family. We got a bulletin down here 'bout it after it happened. I forgot 'bout this Acadia LaFleur we got here. Like I say, she ain't been around in years, but when I realized the connection, I gave ole Sheriff Roy a call—you know, 'cause of it bein' the same name and all. That and the baseball bat."

Dimase nodded. He remembered that yesterday, Sheriff Roy had said the weapon was a bat, the same weapon they assumed the attacker had used in the Alexandria attack. "What about the baseball bat?"

"The guy left it right there on the floor, covered with blood and such."

"Where is the bat now?" Dimase asked.

"The state police took it to send to their lab."

"I see," Dimase said. "Do you think I could interview the mother and maybe take a ride out to the crime scene?"

"Sure thing, Detective. I'll have to tag along, but we can do that. I cleared my schedule. Sheriff Roy said you the real deal, son. I guess we gonna find out."

CHAPTER 12

Sheriff DeWitt and Dimase jumped into the sheriff's cruiser and rode together the few blocks to the rooming house where the victim's mother had been placed. "Anna LaFleur is her name," DeWitt said. "She knows we're comin'. The doc gave her some pills yesterday to calm her down. We'll see how she's doin' today. We'll meet with her, maybe have a coffee, and see what she can tell us."

The sheriff parked his cruiser in front of a turn-of-the-century Victorian-style home, and he and Dimase knocked and entered. The elderly woman who owned the boardinghouse showed them into the parlor. Anna LaFleur was seated in an old upholstered armchair with a blanket covering her lower body. Dimase had noted in the police file that she was only fifty years old, but the woman in front of them looked at least seventy. She had straight, thin, shoulder-length white hair brushed straight back. Her face was extremely wrinkled, and when she smiled, her teeth were yellow and crooked. Her features were thick, and her head seemed to sit directly on her shoulders, with a turkey-like gullet camouflaging any sign of a neck.

She didn't get up when Dimase and the sheriff entered the room; instead, she raised a gnarled, age-spotted hand in a slight gesture to acknowledge their presence. There was no light in her eyes. The

STEPHEN L BRUNEAU

woman gave every appearance of someone who had been beaten down by life.

"Good mawnin', Miss Anna," the sheriff said. "This here is Detective Augustin. He's gonna help us find out who did this to your girl. He has to ask you a few questions. Is that all right?"

Anna nodded and motioned to the coffee table, where the landlady had left a tray with a freshly brewed pot of coffee and the requisite accessories. Taking the hint, Dimase poured a cup for the sheriff and for himself and freshened the cup Anna had on the small table beside her.

"Miss Anna," Dimase said, addressing her in the same manner as a local, "did you ever hear from your daughter during the years when she was away?"

"Yes," she replied in a gravelly voice hoarse from crying or smoking or both. "She was a good daughter, Detective. She took care of her mama. She was a good girl."

"Do you know where she lived during those years? Did she ever come home to visit?"

"No." Anna shook her head sadly. "She never came back home till this last time. Now I'm sorry she did. She wrote me letters every single month, and she always sent money. She would tell me about all the excitin' and famous people she was workin' with. I used to love to read the letters. It made me so happy that she was doin' good."

"Where was she living during this time?" Dimase repeated. "What type of work was she doing?"

"She was in Washington, DC, the whole time, almost ten years since she left home. She was a tour guide. She worked for some really fancy company. She said they only worked with famous or important people, and when they came to town, it was her job to show them around—you know, the monuments and museums and such. She met all kinds of excitin' people. I guess she even dated some of 'em from time to time. I always hoped she might marry one of 'em someday and give me some grandkids, and we could all live together someplace nice. That ain't gonna happen now."

Anna started to tear up, and Dimase quickly pressed on. "Tell me. These letters—do you still have them? How many are there?"

70

"Oh, them is my most prized possession," Anna replied. "I kept every one of 'em. There's over a hundred—one for every month she was away. She never forgot her mama. Like I say, Detective, she was a good girl."

"Where are the letters now?" Dimase asked. "Would you let me look at them? There must be something in them that would give us a clue."

The woman's lips twisted into a crooked half smile through her tears. "I told you—they is my prized possession. You can look through them if it will help find who done this to her, but you cain't take them away from me. Me and Cady—that's my name fo' her—was lookin' through them just the other day, laughin' and rememberin', and she was tellin' me stories about some of the people she wrote about. I got a steel box with a lock. I keep it under my bed. If the place ever burn down, them letters is the one thing I don't ever want to lose."

"If I can just take the box for a short time and maybe make some copies, I promise to return them as soon as I can and exactly as I found them. How would I unlock the box?" Dimase could see that the woman was wavering. He smiled encouragingly and spread his palms in a gesture of supplication.

"They's a key in the top drawer of my nightstand, way in the back, underneath a bunch of stuff."

"Thank you, Miss Anna," Dimase said. "We're going to go now. I'm very sorry for your loss. We will find the person who did this to your daughter—I promise you. We will talk again."

Back in the police cruiser, Sheriff DeWitt asked, "Where to?"

"Let's not waste any time," Dimase replied. "I want to see what's in those letters. Sounds like they should still be there, right? Your boys didn't take them. What about the state police?"

"Naw, I don't think so. Like I said, they took pictures and did some stuff to the body before it got taken away. They took the baseball bat, but I don't think they took nuthin' else."

"All right then, let's check it out."

Sheriff Dewitt looked at Dimase with a wide grin and hit the siren and flashers. They covered the seventeen miles to Sugartown in fifteen minutes. Amid vast fields of melons on either side of Route 112, they turned off onto a dusty dirt road and, within a couple hundred feet, came to the crumbling wooden structure that was Anna LaFleur's home. Dimase couldn't help but notice the contrast in living conditions from the LaFleurs in Alexandria. "I wonder if there is any relation to our Acadia LaFleur's branch of the family."

"I doubt it," the sheriff replied. "Nuthin' that matters anyway; I imagine we is all related if you go back far enough. Maybe they is distant cousins or sumthin', but they is plenty of LaFleurs in Louisiana, and they proly don't know about each other."

The front door was unlocked, so Dimase pushed it in and ducked under the yellow police tape draped across the doorframe. The bend was a little too much for Sheriff DeWitt, so he simply ripped the tape down and followed Dimase in. The interior was a mess, partly due to what had transpired recently but more so because of how the old lady lived. Clutter was everywhere, with dishes stacked in the sink and trash bags holding all kinds of different objects scattered about the space. There was one longer room that served as both a kitchen and a living area. Down a short hallway were two bedrooms and a small bathroom.

Dimase and DeWitt stepped carefully around a chalk outline on the floor where Cady LaFleur's body had fallen. There were dark blood stains and debris everywhere. "It looks like she may have put up a fight," Dimase said, carefully avoiding the overturned table and shards of glass scattered on the floor. He got down on his hands and knees, carefully examining the shattered glass. "This glass is from that lamp over there," he said, pointing across the room. "I wonder how it got all the way over here. Look at the spray pattern of the pieces."

"What are you thinkin'?" Sheriff DeWitt asked, scratching his head with a look of puzzlement on his face.

"Look at it this way," Dimase said as he continued to examine the glass piece by piece. "If the table was upended and the lamp fell, the glass would be near the table. The base of the lamp is near where the body fell, yet the glass from the casing is way over here on the other side of the room, arrayed in a crescent-moon pattern. The shards are too far away and too spread out for the casing to have broken where the lamp fell. And how did the base of the lamp get all the way from the table to where the body fell?"

"I don't know," DeWitt said, scratching his head.

Dimase stood, angling his body as a batter would have toward a baseball. "The attacker had a baseball bat in his hands. Maybe the victim picked up the lamp and tried to use it to defend herself. She must have hit him up high, because if she'd missed or just dropped the lamp, the glass would be over there by the body. Picture the victim swinging the lamp at her attacker and hitting him in the head. Where would you expect the glass to lie?"

"Proly over there," the sheriff said, pointing. "All spread out like it is."

"Exactly!" Dimase exclaimed. He suddenly bent down. "And here is what I've been looking for." He held up a jagged finger-sized piece of the shattered lamp casing. "Do you see the slight stains on the tip and edge of this piece? I believe this is the attacker's blood, not the victim's."

"Well, I'll be damned," the sheriff replied. "I guess Sheriff Roy was right about you. What are you going to do with it?"

Dimase took a small baggie from his pocket and sealed the glass inside. "I'm going to make arrangements to ship it to the FBI lab. We'll notify the state police and keep everything above board, but they had their chance at the crime scene. The FBI has the best lab in the world. Let's see what they come up with, and we'll cover our butts by letting the state police know about it right after I ship it off."

"They might not like that," DeWitt said.

"Perhaps not, but they'll get over it. In the end, it will help their investigation, and we wouldn't be withholding anything from them. They've got the baseball bat, but my guess is the perp wore gloves, so they are not going to get any prints. The only blood on the bat is going to be from the victim. From what you say, it sounds like they took fluid and tissue from the victim, but unless the attacker bled on her, I don't think they're looking at anything that might have his DNA. This little piece of glass could be the key to tying someone to the crime once we have a suspect."

"Sounds like a plan," DeWitt said. "I'll go along with you all right."

"Good. Let's see if we can take a look at those letters," Dimase said, getting to his feet.

In the back bedroom, beneath the bed, they found the steel box exactly where Anna LaFleur had said it would be. Sheriff DeWitt found the key in the nightstand drawer, and together they opened the box. Inside was a pile of handwritten letters unfolded and stacked in chronological order, with the most recent on top. There were dozens of letters, all in excellent condition. Dimase carefully removed them, placing the letters on the bed.

In the box, beneath the letters was something else. It was a small diary-type notebook. Dimase opened it and scanned the pages. The diary went back more than ten years, and the pages were filled with a neat, feminine cursive script. He read a few lines and realized it had belonged to Acadia LaFleur. "Look at this," Dimase said. "I wonder how it got in here with the letters."

"Her mama didn't say nothing about a diary. She may not even know it was in the box." DeWitt pondered for a moment. "Her ma, Miss Anna, said they were readin' the letters together the other day. Maybe when they was done, young Cady stuck the diary in there 'cause she didn't want no one to find it. Maybe she was hidin' somethin'."

Dimase started from the back of the diary, looking at the most recent entries. "Look at this. Her last entry was made one week ago. It says she's happy to be home, and she wishes her ma was feeling better, but this is the only place she feels safe right now."

Dimase flipped through a few more pages. "Look what she wrote two weeks ago."

> Something is wrong with Dickie. He didn't want to meet at our usual time last week. I asked him what was wrong, and he said I need to learn to mind my own business, and I'd better watch my back and not be so nosy. That's not like Dickie at all. He's usually really happy to see me and always very nice. I wish I had never seen that text! It was something about some guy dying

and some operation on his scotis, whatever that is. I didn't really get it, but Dickie changed the minute he got that text, and he seemed none too pleased that I saw it. Now he almost seems threatening. He sounded like he meant it when he said to watch my back and mind my own business. It's making me feel scared. Dickie is one of the most important people in Washington, and all his friends are important too. I don't know what was in that text that he didn't want me to see, but something made him mad at me, I think. I'm going to get out of town for a while—go home and visit Mama. It's time I should see her anyway. I don't think anyone will bother me there. Whatever is wrong will probably blow over in a few weeks.

Dimase closed the diary. "She was running from something. I wonder who Dickie is. He could be the key to the whole thing. It's like she is speaking to us from the grave."

"I wonder what an operation on your scotis is," DeWitt said. "I never heard of such a thing."

"I don't know either," Dimase replied. "We've got to take the letters and diary and read through every word. Maybe we'll find some more references to Dickie or something else that will help us. Let's take this stuff back to your office. Do you have a place where we can spread this all out and go through it?"

"Sure do. We got a conference room with a big ole table. The boys usually eat lunch in there, but I'll tell 'em they got to eat somewhere else till we is done with this here case."

"Good," Dimase replied. "Let's get back there and get started. I also need to ship this glass fragment off to Bill Larson to see if we've got anything on it we can work with."

CHAPTER
13

Washington, DC

Senator Monroe and Ben Johnson exited the restaurant together. The meeting had gone well from Monroe's perspective. Ben Johnson was a significant player and would be a good ally to have long term. Although Johnson obviously tried to play his politics straight down the middle, Monroe thought that might be a good thing to a point. To the extent Monroe could get him to play ball, using Johnson's company as a primary government contractor could be spun as being both inclusive and nonpartisan. It didn't hurt politically that his company was one of the largest and most successful minority-owned businesses in the country.

Monroe was not worried about Fischer, Forbes, and Johnson's ability to evolve as a company. Any hiccups along the way could easily be washed away by the tidal wave of federal money that would roll over the country for the next twenty years. The real question was whether Johnson would play ball, or was he too much of a straight arrow? Thus far, Monroe had not probed too deeply into that question. That day's lunch meeting had been to get acquainted and set the stage. Johnson and his company were a good fit in many respects, but to make the relationship work in the way Monroe envisioned for the long run, Johnson would have to become one of them.

The two men shook hands on the sidewalk and agreed to meet again within the next week or two. Monroe waved as Johnson slid into the backseat of his waiting limo, and the driver pulled away. Monroe had instructed his own driver to stay away and instead hailed a cab, once again ordering the cabbie to take him to Arlington National Cemetery. Harrington had updates.

At Arlington, he found Harrington in the same general area, near Robert E. Lee's old farmhouse, and the two men strolled separately to an isolated alcove where they sat near each other on a pair of stone benches centered in the garden.

"Your little problem with the hooker is taken care of," Harrington said softly.

"Good," Monroe replied. "I don't want to know any details."

"I won't tell you specifics, but there was a fuckup. You're probably going to hear about it sooner or later, so I'm just giving you a heads-up."

"What kind of fuckup?" Monroe asked.

"The job got pushed down several levels. It was outsourced to a local thug. That way, even if something goes wrong and he gets caught, there's no tie back to us—no conspiracy."

"I get it," the senator said impatiently. "So what's the problem?"

"I'm getting to that," Harrington replied. "It worked a little bit like that kids' game telephone. You ever play that game?"

"What the fuck are you talking about, Frank?"

"You know, everyone sits in a circle, and you whisper something to the person next to you, and by the time the message gets all the way around the circle, the whole phrase has changed around."

"Enough of the bullshit," Monroe hissed. "What happened?"

"The good news is that, like I said, the network is well protected up and down the chain of command. No one would ever connect it to any of us. The bad news is that the orders to take out the hooker, and the background information on her, were kept vague at every level. No one wanted to specifically say, 'Take this person out at this address,' and give a specific order. By the time it got to the local numb-nuts who

78

was actually going to do the job, it got too vague. All he took from his instruction was that Washington wanted to take out Acadia LaFleur, and he had to find her and get it done."

"So what's the problem?" Monroe said again irritably.

"Do you know how many Acadia LaFleurs there are in Louisiana? There's actually quite a few. We found out that was the real name of your hooker. We got word she went back to Louisiana. By the time the order got to the local guy, he didn't know anything about her being a hooker or how old she was. He was asked if he knew an Acadia LaFleur with connections to Washington. He said yes. He was told Washington didn't want her around anymore and to take care of it. Turned out he knew the wrong Acadia LaFleur. He took out the wrong woman."

"Are you shitting me?" Monroe felt as if he were going to explode, and it took everything he had not to make a scene that would draw attention to them. "Are we working with a bunch of morons? How could this guy be so stupid? I thought you said the hooker was dead."

"She is," Harrington replied. "She won't be an issue anymore. Our guy mistakenly attacked a woman with the same name. When we figured out what had happened, we sent word down and pointed him back in the right direction, and two weeks later, he finished the job. That's why your hooker is no longer a problem."

"Jesus H. Christ!" the senator exclaimed. "We don't need distractions like this. Are your people competent enough to take out the right target in the main operation?"

"Don't worry," Harrington said. "That process is being well managed by top professionals. Louisiana was a side job—a side job made necessary because of you, I might add. There is one other thing."

Monroe's jaw dropped, and he glared at Frank.

"The Acadia LaFleur who got attacked the first time—she's tied to one of us. You know her brother-in-law. He's a congressman, Francois LaFleur. Her husband is Alphonse LaFleur. He's an aide to his brother, the congressman. The woman didn't die. She's in a coma. It doesn't look good for her."

Monroe was beside himself. It had been a simple job! "How could things get so completely fucked up?"

"Calm down," Harrington said. "The congressman has no idea. They think it's a random home invasion gone wrong." He kept his voice low. "It was a colossal screwup, but no harm, no foul. It doesn't affect the operation. No connections to operation SCOTUS. Everything is in place and on time. Unfortunately, the congressman's sister-in-law is just collateral damage."

"What about the local bozo who screwed it all up? Is he a threat to identify any of our people or compromise us in any way?"

"I don't think so. We'll monitor the situation and take corrective action if warranted."

"What about the Acadia LaFleur in a coma? If she comes out of it, can she identify your local muscle? That puts the squeeze on him. If he gives up your guy, then they put the squeeze on him and try to keep working their way back up the chain."

"Same thing," Harrington said. "I don't think so. We'll monitor the situation and take corrective action if warranted."

Monroe just shook his head. "You'd better be right, Frank." He turned and walked away.

CHAPTER
14

Deridder, Louisiana

D imase and DeWitt were holed up in the conference room of the Deridder Sheriff's Department for the better part of a week, poring through young Cady LaFleur's letters to her mom and reviewing her personal diary. DeWitt seemed pleased to be part of what felt like a real investigation, although after several long days of painstaking analysis, the novelty was starting to wear off.

The room was strewn with empty pizza boxes, sub wrappers, and Styrofoam coffee cups. Most of the food trash belonged to DeWitt; more of the cups belonged to Dimase. DeWitt was steadfast about not allowing Dimase to smoke, so every couple hours, Dimase took a smoke break out behind the building. Subsisting mainly on coffee and cigarettes was his habit when immersed in a case. He knew it wasn't true, but he rationalized that he could think more clearly when he limited food intake and heightened his senses with nicotine and caffeine. DeWitt, on the other hand, seemed to think he did his best work with a mouthful of pizza.

True to his word, Dimase notified the Louisiana State Police about the small glass piece from the lamp casing, right after he shipped it off to Larson for processing at the FBI. The state cops were none too happy about it but came around a bit when Dimase pointed out that they were finished at the crime scene, and technically, the case was under DeWitt's jurisdiction, so it was his choice as to which resources to use in regard to any follow-up evidence.

Dimase had Bill Larson ask the FBI to do whatever they could to expedite the testing of the glass shard for DNA. He also requested they try to match up whatever they found on the glass with the result from the partial fingernail he'd sent to them a week earlier. Then they had to find out whom the DNA belonged to.

At Dimase's request, in addition to staying on top of the DNA analysis, back in Boston, Bill Larson also employed the considerable resources of Augustin and Larson Confidential LLC to put together a comprehensive background dossier on the younger Acadia LaFleur, a.k.a. Daisy May, which he emailed to Dimase. On his way back from a smoke break, Dimase took the PDF from the printer just outside the conference room and scanned the highlights.

As a girl, Cady had grown up in the same ramshackle home where she'd died just days ago. There had been no father in the picture. She and her mom had subsisted on welfare and part-time cash jobs in nearby Deridder. By the time Cady was eighteen, she'd found work as an exotic dancer in a gentlemen's club located in a neighboring parish. Eventually, she'd been recruited to dance on a circuit of similar clubs up and down the East Coast, from Bangor, Maine, to Washington, DC. She'd been young and beautiful. The opportunity to make even more cash had become self-evident over time, and for the past several years, she'd worked exclusively in Washington for an elite prostitution ring known as Premiere Escort Service.

In DC, Cady had had a lavishly furnished condo located in an upscale section of Columbia Heights and a bank account with a balance of more than $300,000. No list of clients had been found, but the Premiere Escort Service had a reputation as one of the most selective, discreet, high-end operations in a city that could easily have been considered the most concentrated center of power in the United States. It was rumored that the service's clientele consisted of some of the biggest names in Washington, a who's who of the wealthy and connected.

Cady's professional persona had been Daisy May, likely a play on her rural roots. Her online profile at Premiere Escort had been taken down. The authorities in DC did not appear to be looking for her. Apparently, the Louisiana State Police had not yet connected the dots to her life in Washington, DC. Larson had sent a couple operatives out to go through her condo, but they hadn't come up with anything new. In fact, Larson had related to Dimase that he suspected her place had been scrubbed.

Interestingly, no computer or cell phone had been found in her unit. Dimase could understand the no cell phone part. She probably had taken it with her when she left, but no computer, no printer, and no wires hanging from the wall? Dimase wondered about the computer. Everyone had a computer in that day and age, did they not?

"Sheriff," Dimase said, "do we know what happened to her cell phone? She must have had a cell phone. Do you know if the state police took it?"

Sheriff DeWitt contemplated an hours-old piece of pizza crust and began to nibble at the end. "Now that you mention it, I don't recall that comin' up. I signed a release for them to take whatever they took from the scene. I don't recall no cell phone."

"That's rather peculiar, don't you think? Everyone has a cell phone, especially someone in her line of work."

"Well," the sheriff said, "I reckon maybe the perp took it with him or maybe threw it into the swamp or sumpin', probably a long way from Sugartown. Maybe they is sumthin' on there they don't want no one to see."

Dimase considered that. "I believe you are right. Whatever made her come back here has to do with one of her clients. I'm betting on this Dickie guy with the phone text she saw. He's the key, whoever he is. That has to be it. She was running. Why? She saw something or heard something she wasn't supposed to. That's my guess. We may never find her phone, but I think someone wanted her dead for something she knew—something she saw on someone else's phone. Why all of a sudden, after all those years in DC, did someone want her dead, and what the hell does it have to do with the Acadia LaFleur in a coma in Alexandria?"

CHAPTER
15

Alexandria, Louisiana

The Thursday night crowd at Billy Ray's Bar was a tough one, but that was no different from any other night. The flavor was distinctively redneck. A Confederate flag hung behind the bar, and pictures of Civil War generals, from Robert E. Lee to Stonewall Jackson, hung among posters of several generations of country singers.

Despite the local ordinance to the contrary, smoking was informally allowed, as the sheriff's department generally gave the place a wide berth unless they were forced to go down and break up a fight, which usually happened about once a week. The clientele consisted of an assortment of bikers, laborers, farmers, a few other versions of southern hillbillies, and skinheads. Denim, leather, and beards were the uniform of choice for the nonconformists seeking to conform to each other.

Rufus Manteau was busy pouring drinks behind the bar and clearly not in a mood for conversation. Foul-natured anyway, he was particularly irritable that night and not going to take shit from anyone. Of course, that was why he had the job in the first place—because

Rufus had a reputation, and only a crazy person would have thought about giving Rufus shit.

He wasn't the biggest man in the room, but everyone knew that when Rufus went off, one didn't want to get in the way. More than one patron had been carried out of the bar bloody, beaten, and missing a few teeth. It was a natural fit that a bar with that type of clientele needed a guy like Rufus to maintain law and order street style.

Those days, Rufus had a lot on his mind, and he wasn't the type to be able to set aside whatever was bothering him. To the contrary, Rufus was wound a bit tightly, which was a plus when it came to maintaining discipline in the bar but a minus in terms of managing his own anxiety. If Rufus had a problem, it tended to fester, ramping up his anxiety in a vicious circle of escalating tension.

As he pulled the tap, filling a beer mug, and placed the mug on the bar for the biker in front of him, his fingers moved unconsciously to his bandage. He wondered if he'd have a permanent scar from that young bitch hitting him with the lamp and the other one up in Alexandria slicing him with her fingernail. More than that, he wondered if the older one would ever come out of her coma.

He'd seen stuff like that on TV—someone was in a coma for months or even years, and all of a sudden, he or she woke up and started talking. That could be a real problem if it happened in this case. The bitch had been quicker than he'd thought for an old broad, and she'd gouged him pretty well before he spun her around and knocked her down the stairs. He knew she had seen him in that moment—just for an instant, but they had been face-to-face. The look in her eyes had been something. She had known she was going to die—only she hadn't died. He wished he'd gone down the stairs and finished the job, but he'd figured she was done and had wanted to get the hell out of there.

What a stupid dumbass he was. To make matters worse, then he'd found out he'd gone after the wrong woman, and he'd had to do the whole thing all over again down in Sugartown. At least that bitch wouldn't be talking anymore. She had been a fighter too, a lot younger than the first one. She actually had ducked his first swing and hit him upside the head with a lamp before he jabbed her in the jaw with the butt end of the bat. That had sent her to the floor, where that time, he'd made sure he ended it.

The wound was still fresh on the side of his head, but he'd covered it up with a large bandage beside his eye. One of the regulars slid next to his pal at the bar and smiled at Rufus. "What happened to you, brother? Your ole lady pop you one?"

Rufus gave him a menacing look and walked away. He was tempted to grab the bat beneath the bar and wave it in the guy's face but resisted the urge.

Bats were his weapon of choice. They were perfect for bar enforcement, unless a guy pulled a gun on him. He had a wide assortment of a half dozen lengths and weights, hidden from view, leaning against the wall. His collection was one short since he'd left one at the shack in Sugartown the other night. Unlike the first time, when he'd taken the bat with him, the second time, he'd opted to wear gloves and just leave the bat at the scene. Why risk driving back to Alexandria with bloody evidence in the car or having someone see him dispose of it?

Rufus had another secret that no one else in the bar was aware of. For the past two years, he had been a low-level informer to the FBI. The extra money was good, and he never gave them anything too sweet. He really didn't have anything high level to give them. He was just a cog in their network, providing background when asked or passing on scuttlebutt and street talk from the criminal element who frequented Billy Ray's. One time about a year ago, he'd pointed his handler in the direction of a cigarette-smuggling ring, and no one was the wiser. That tip had brought in a nice little bonus.

The last time around had been the first time they'd asked him to do something to anyone. It hadn't seemed like part of a legal operation, but the money had been good, and he'd assumed they would have his back. Now he was none too sure.

His handler had not been happy when he'd found out Rufus had taken out the wrong Acadia LaFleur. How had Rufus been supposed to know? The handler had asked only if he knew a local woman named Acadia LaFleur with connections to Washington, DC. Hell yes, he knew her. "Good," the handler had said. "She's become a problem that needs to go away. Will ten grand make her go away?"

"Hell yes," he'd said. "Hell yes."

Now she was a problem that wouldn't go away. The more Rufus's brain got churning, the more amped up he became; the anxiety rose within him like mercury in a thermometer. If she woke up from her coma and started talking, he might be toast.

Then he looked at the situation from a different angle that sent a shiver through his body. His handler obviously had no issue with solving problems by making people go away. What if his handler decided the simplest solution to the problem was to make Rufus go away? If Rufus was gone, the old lady could wake up and talk all she wanted, and the handler and his people would be perfectly safe.

She might identify Rufus, but that was where her story would end. There would be no connection to the handler or anyone else. Dead men told no tales. That thought sent another chill down Rufus's spine. For all he knew, he might have been on the clock right now. After all, it was the FBI, for Chrissakes. They could pretty much do anything they wanted to.

The more Rufus thought about it, the more obvious it became. There was only one solution that made sense from the FBI's standpoint: to make Rufus go away, just as they'd asked him to make Acadia LaFleur go away.

Rufus looked around the bar. Paranoia was starting to set in. No one looked out of the ordinary, but then again, they wouldn't have, would they? There was only one way out: he had to finish the job. If Acadia LaFleur never woke up, then the chain would stop with her, and Rufus would no longer be a risk to the FBI. Rufus made a decision. He was painted into a corner. It would be ballsy, but he had to get Acadia LaFleur, and the sooner the better.

CHAPTER 16

Deridder, Louisiana

Dimase Augustin tossed and turned in his bed at the motel outside Deridder. Sleep eluded him. Passages from the diary and letters streamed through his mind, but one in particular kept coming back to him: "Dickie gave me diamond earrings last week for my birthday. Gonna see him at the Gate tomorrow, and I'm going to make it really special for him."

What does it mean? he wondered. *Nothing foreboding about it.*

In the past week, Dimase had read through Cady LaFleurs's letters to her mom three times. There were 123 letters. Some were longer than others, but all were at least two pages, and a few were much longer. Dimase had done a quick count. In all, there were 280 pages, sprinkled with references to famous people, most of whom were not specifically named. Cady had included quite a few of her own made-up nicknames or, in some cases, mentioned an occupation or position and occasionally a description of the person or circumstance.

He lay back on the bed and pulled the covers over his head. The diary was another three hundred pages long. Dimase had scoured the diary pages and letters for any other reference to someone called Dickie, but other than the one about the diamond earrings and, later, the one about his anger over the text, the name didn't appear.

Dickie at the Gate. Who the hell is Dickie, and what is the Gate? Dimase drifted in and out of restless semisleep. All of a sudden, his eyes popped open, and he sat bolt upright, fully awake. "Watergate," he said out loud. There was one other reference to Watergate he remembered. He didn't think there was any nickname attached to the passage and certainly not the nickname Dickie. He would have remembered that, but *Gate* clearly referred to a place, a place where she was going to see Dickie, who had given her diamond earrings for her birthday, the next day. The Watergate made perfect sense. He had to look at that passage again.

Dimase got dressed as fast as he could and lit a cigarette. It was five o'clock in the morning, so he didn't bother to call Sheriff Dewitt, who he was sure would still be sleeping. The night sergeant would let him in.

Dimase ran up the front steps of the sheriff's department. The door was locked, but the desk sergeant recognized him and buzzed him in. "Going to the conference room," Dimase said breathlessly. "Just thought of something I have to check out."

The sergeant waved him past, and Dimase went back to the conference room and started leafing through the stack of letters. He knew it wasn't a recent letter, so he started about six months back and worked backward from there. He scanned pages quickly but carefully, using the retracted tip of a pen to help keep himself on line and maintain a fast pace.

He found what he was looking for after about fifteen minutes. The letter was dated almost exactly fifteen months ago: "I met a senator today. He lives at Watergate—you know, famous for Richard Nixon and all that. Pretty cool, huh, Ma? So many famous and important people around here." After that paragraph, the letter went on to an unrelated topic. Dimase was confident that was the only other reference to Watergate in all the letters and diary entries he'd read through so many times—the only reference, that was, other than

Cady's diary entries in which she mentioned seeing Dickie at the Gate and seeing the text on Dickie's phone.

When DeWitt came in, the two of them would have to spend the next few hours going through all the written material one more time, looking for any additional references to Watergate or the Gate. Dimase was confident there were none, but he had to be sure. If he was right, Dickie and the senator could be the same person. Whoever the senator was, he clearly had lived or stayed at Watergate at some point. There was no doubt in Dimase's mind that "the Gate" referred to Watergate. If, in all the letters and diary entries, there was no other mention of Watergate, was it not reasonable to surmise that Dickie at the Gate might, in fact, be the senator?

It was time to get Bill Larson out of bed back in Boston. Dimase pushed the letters aside and hit his partner up on his cell phone. As he should have known, Larson was already on his way to the gym for his early morning workout. "Bill, I may have something," Dimase said excitedly. "It's not directly related to our Acadia LaFleur in Alexandria, but I may have a lead on why Cady LaFleur, the escort, left Washington. I need you to run something down for me."

"Well, guess what, D-Man?" Larson said. "I have something for you. The preliminary DNA report came back overnight. It's a perfect match between the DNA on the fingernail and the DNA on your piece of glass. There's no doubt about it. The same guy attacked both Acadia LaFleurs. We have no idea who he is or why the hell he went after them, but at least we know for sure the two cases are tied together. Find the connection between the two Acadias, and maybe that will point to your guy."

"That's good news," Dimase replied. "I have no idea at this point what that connection might be, but there has to be something. Sooner or later, we will find it. There is nothing I have seen to indicate they ever knew each other or crossed paths in any way, but we'll keep looking."

"What did you have for me?" Larson asked.

"I'm looking for a senator who has a place in the Watergate apartments. His nickname may be Dick or Dickie. I don't know if he has a place at the Watergate or if he just goes there. Take a look at a list of all the senators. Narrow it down to anyone with a first name or middle name of Richard or Dick. Make some discreet inquiries around the Watergate. Grease some palms. Vet every single senator on that short list for a connection to Watergate. Put a couple of undercover guys at the Watergate if you have to. Give them photos of any senator on that short list. Do deep background on all of them. I think he's the reason she took off. There's a passage near the end of her diary about a text she saw on some guy's phone that made the guy get pissed off. The guy's name was Dickie. We need to find out if the Dickie in her diary is the senator she talked about meeting at Watergate in an earlier letter to her mother. Whatever it was she learned, they chased her all the way to Louisiana and killed her for it. I'm thinking this senator, Dickie, whoever he is, knows why."

CHAPTER 17

Alexandria, Louisiana

By seven o'clock, Rufus couldn't take it anymore. He told the other bartender that he had a pounding headache and felt like he was going to puke and had to go home. The bar was pretty busy, and his coworker was not happy about being left on his own, but Rufus insisted, and the guy acquiesced.

Rufus's description of how he was feeling was not far from the truth. He couldn't wait any longer; his anxiety and lack of impulse control were getting the best of him. He had to finish the job, and he had to finish it now. It was the only way to get himself off the hook with the FBI. Time was of the essence.

Rufus climbed into his old Ford F-150 pickup truck parked behind the bar and immediately took his weed pipe from the glove compartment and sucked in a couple deep tokes to calm his nerves. He had a rough outline of a plan in his head. He needed to get his hands on some flowers in order to gain access to Acadia's hospital room. He wasn't sure how to figure out exactly which room she was in, but he hoped the flowers would do the trick.

The only florist he knew of was already closed for the day, so he went a little out of his way to stop by Walmart to pick up a prepackaged bouquet and a get-well card. He carefully filled out the card, taking pains to make sure the handwriting did not look like his own; sealed the card in the envelope; and tucked it in the top of the flowers.

At the hospital, Rufus parked his truck in the covered parking garage and walked straight into the main entrance to the volunteer manning the information desk. "I have a flower delivery for Miss Acadia LaFleur. Could you please tell me how to find her?"

The woman regarded him curiously, looking him up and down. He did not look like a flower delivery boy, and the flowers looked pretty pathetic, but she directed him to the east elevators and the fourth-floor nurses' station. Rufus could feel the anxiety welling up within him. He wished he'd taken another hit on his pipe right before entering the hospital. His heart was pounding, and his head was swimming.

Rufus hit the call button for the elevator. It seemed to take forever to arrive. His eyes were riveted to the floor indicator lights above the doorframe. Maybe this wasn't such a good idea after all. That bitch at the front desk had already seen his face up close. He wondered if there were security cameras in the parking garage, by the information desk, or in the elevator. Panic and paranoia gripped him.

The elevator doors opened on the fourth floor, and Rufus stepped into the corridor, trying to get his bearings. He saw signs pointing both left and right, indicating different room numbers in each direction. He had no idea which room Acadia LaFleur was in. He felt as if he were going to pass out. Briefly, he considered tossing the flowers into the trash, returning to his truck, and getting the hell out of there.

Not an option, he thought. If he didn't finish the job, he'd be a dead man walking. The numbers on the sign seemed to blur. He picked right, turned the corner, and spotted a nurses' station up ahead. A lone middle-aged woman in a nurse's uniform sat in a chair, working at a computer. Rufus cleared his throat to get her attention. His words came out thick and heavy, not at all as he intended. "Excuse me, ma'am. Could you tell me which room Miss LaFleur is in? I have some flowers to deliver to her."

The woman looked surprised. "You shouldn't be up here," she said. "Visiting hours are over."

"I won't be but a moment, ma'am. I'll just leave them for her and go." Damn, now two women had seen his face. He hadn't really thought through the plan. When he'd left the bar, he'd figured the flowers would get him to her room, and he'd play everything else by ear.

"You can't go to her room," the nurse said firmly. "Leave them here, and I'll see that she gets them."

Faced with no other choice, Rufus relented and left the flowers on the counter. "Ma'am, is there a bathroom I can use before I go?"

"Back toward the elevator. Door on your left," she said, indicating the conversation was over by turning her back to him and returning to her work on the computer.

Rufus headed back down the corridor toward the elevator. He still had no clue which room Acadia was in. He ducked into a gender-neutral restroom and splashed water onto his face, attempting to get his breathing under control. He cracked open the door and peered back at the nurses' station. Within a minute or two, the nurse took the flowers and started walking in the opposite direction, away from him.

Rufus hustled out of the restroom and followed her, keeping his distance and praying she wouldn't turn around and see him. There didn't seem to be anyone else around at the moment. Up ahead, he saw the nurse turn into a room. Rufus ducked into a different patient room one door away and tucked himself into the hanging curtain designed to provide patient privacy. The patient in the bed behind him appeared to be napping.

Rufus forced himself to count to one hundred in order to give the nurse plenty of time to leave the flowers and return to her station. He poked his head out the door and looked both ways to make sure the coast was clear. The patient behind him stirred awake and called out, "Hey, who are you? What are you doing here?"

Rufus turned and gave the man the quiet sign by putting his finger to his lips. Rufus realized he did not look like an orderly or a nurse. The man continued to raise a ruckus.

"Why were you hiding in my curtain? What the hell is going on?"

Rufus shut the door tightly and faced the man, motioning with his palms for the man to calm down and be quiet. The man reached for some sort of a control on a cord hanging from his bed, and Rufus realized it was a call button. Without hesitation, he rushed across the room, grabbed a pillow, and jammed it tightly against the man's face. The patient let out a series of muffled cries, but within seconds, he went quiet as Rufus forced his full weight on the pillow. The man feebly tried to grasp at the pillow, but Rufus was too strong. The man's legs and feet twitched violently before his arms fell weakly to his sides, and then all movement ceased.

Rufus removed the pillow and tucked it in with the others that were supporting the man's head. On the cord hanging from the bed, Rufus noticed the call button was flashing. Damn, the man had hit the button before Rufus could get to him. Help was on the way.

He cracked the door to the corridor once again, just in time to see the nurse come from behind her station and start toward him. There was a new development as well: to his left, at the opposite end of the corridor, a janitor had appeared and was busy buffing the floor with an automatic machine. The man looked as if he'd just retired from the NFL. He had his back to Rufus and wore a pair of headphones. The guy was enormous, at least six foot five and probably more than three hundred pounds. His triceps bulged as he guided the buffing machine back and forth in a systematic pattern over the tiles.

Through the narrow opening, Rufus directed his attention back to the nurse, who was still walking toward him. She had her head down, reading something on a clipboard she held in her hand. He shut the door, retreated across the room, and took refuge in the lavatory, leaving the door cracked so he could hear what was going on and perhaps catch a glimpse. Rufus's heart pounded in his chest. He felt as if he were having heart attack.

The nurse entered the room and called out the patient's name as she went to his bed. Rufus could hear her and see her back as she examined the patient. "Oh dear!" she exclaimed. "Mr. Clyde, can you hear me?" She shook the patient gently and appeared to check his pulse.

Rufus lurked behind the door, uncertain what to do next.

The nurse took a walkie-talkie from the pocket of her uniform and screamed, "Code blue, room 412! Stat! Repeat: code blue, room 412."

Rufus wasn't sure, but he had a feeling all hell was about to break loose. He burst from behind the lavatory door and grabbed the nurse from behind. Rufus was a powerful man, and the nurse was no match for him. He locked his right arm around her neck and pulled on his right wrist with his left hand, applying maximum pressure and torque.

When he was finished, he dragged her lifeless body into the lavatory and shut the door. He had been upset earlier that three people had seen his face; now two of them were dead. Once again, he slivered the door to the hallway open. The large black janitor was now working the floor right in front of the door to the room he figured Acadia LaFleur was in. To his right, at the far end of the corridor, a man and a woman, both wearing medical smocks, were racing toward him. He was out of time.

Rufus ran back to the lavatory, grabbed a large towel, and quickly wrapped it around his head. He was in all-out panic-driven survival mode. He peeked into the hallway again. The janitor was just feet to his left with his head down, working his machine; his body moved slightly to whatever music was on his headphones. To his right, the two medical personnel were almost upon him.

Rufus burst from the room and ran past the startled janitor. At the far end of the corridor were an exit sign and stairwell. Rufus took the steps two at a time down to the lobby.

The lobby was empty except for the lone volunteer at the information desk. Rufus ran toward her with a maniacal look on the portion of his face that was visible beneath the towel. The woman backed up instinctively, but Rufus was on her in seconds. He brought her to the floor, hunching over so that if there were security cameras, they wouldn't get a good look at him, oblivious to the fact that it was probably too late to worry about that. He made quick work of the helpless woman and ran for the exit, keeping the towel on his head and a raised arm in front of his eyes.

He fired up the engine to his truck, maneuvered out of his parking space, and sped toward the exit. He remembered the parking ticket and pulled it from his shirt pocket before realizing he was supposed to pay at an autopay station back in the lobby. *Shit.* Nothing had gone right that night. He accelerated and crashed through the wooden gate at the parking lot exit, throwing the towel into the backseat as he put the pedal to the metal. He rocked back and forth in the driver's seat, subconsciously trying to calm the adrenaline that surged through his system.

Rufus knew he was fucked. Three people were dead, and not one of them was named Acadia LaFleur. He'd just made things ten times worse. Now the FBI would really be after him. The only good thing was that all three people who had seen his face that night were dead. He knew the cops may or may not catch up to him for what had happened that night, but it wasn't the cops who scared the shit out of him. It was the FBI. They were sure to figure out what had gone down, and they weren't going to like it. He had to get out of town fast. If he didn't make himself disappear, the FBI would do it for him.

CHAPTER
18

Deridder, Louisiana

Dimase figured he'd stay one last night in Deridder and then head back to Alexandria in the morning. For the time being, he'd done as much as he could on that end of the case. In the space of a few days, they had been able to establish definitively that the same person was responsible for the attacks on both Acadia LaFleurs. The DNA match confirmed what circumstantial evidence and the MO had indicated all along. Whoever the perpetrator was, they were closing in on him, and Dimase knew it was only a matter of time before his identity came to light. He made a mental note to call Ben Johnson later in the day to bring him up to speed.

He still didn't have a clear motive in either attack, but both cases seemed to have a Washington connection. Circumstantial evidence supported the theory that young Cady had fled Washington in a hurry to return to Louisiana. Hopefully Larson would come up with some names of senators who might fit the nickname Dickie, and they could shift the focus of their investigation to DC. The picture was still foggy, but Dimase felt if they found the motive behind the Sugartown Cady

LaFleur murder, it might reveal the reason behind the attack on the elder Acadia as well.

Dimase stretched and rolled over, determined to doze for another twenty minutes to catch up on some of the sleep he'd missed over the past week. Just as he was about to drift off, his phone started buzzing. He could see from the caller ID that it was Sheriff Roy from Alexandria. "Good morning," Dimase said, answering the call.

"Ain't nuthin' good about it!" Roy shouted back through the phone. "All hell's broke loose up here. You need to get your ass back up here pronto. I don't know what in the bejesus is goin' on."

"What happened?"

"What happened?" Roy repeated. "I got dead bodies turning up all over the damn hospital last night; that's what happened."

Dimase was instantly awake. "Dead bodies? Who? How? Is Miss Acadia all right?"

"Yeah, she's still the same, but the patient in the room next to her ain't so good. He's dead, and they found a dead nurse in the guy's bathroom."

"In the room next to Acadia LaFleur," Dimase said in disbelief.

Sheriff Roy sounded as if he were hyperventilating. "Did I stutter? Yeah, can you believe that shit? I've never even heard of a case like this, and that ain't all. The volunteer lady at the information desk in the lobby is dead too, lyin' right there on the floor with a broken neck."

"Holy shit." That was all Dimase could manage to say as he processed the information for a moment. "Are there any witnesses or footage?"

"The state police are here now. They're pulling security footage as we speak, and we got three eyewitnesses."

"Good," Dimase said, regaining his composure. "What did they see?"

"It's the damnedest thing. The dead nurse made an emergency call from her walkie-talkie for a code blue. She was in the room next to Acadia LaFleur. Code blue means a patient needs to be resuscitated. There's a skeleton crew working night shift at the hospital, but a doctor and a nurse came runnin' in response to the call. Just before they got to the room, a guy burst out the door, wearing a towel wrapped around his head, and sprinted to the stairwell. When they entered the room, they found the patient dead, and then a couple minutes later, they found the nurse who made the call dead in the lavatory. There was also a night janitor buffing the floor, but none of them got a good look at the guy."

"This is most perplexing," Dimase said. "Why would all this occur in the room next to Acadia LaFleur, yet she is untouched?" He held the phone under his neck as he pulled on his trousers. He didn't believe in coincidences. Clearly, the latest murders were related to Acadia— but how?

"It makes no sense to me," Sheriff Roy replied.

"All right," Dimase said. "I was done here for the time being anyway. I'm on my way. What's going on right now?"

"The place is crawlin' with state police and forensics guys. My guys have set up a perimeter."

"Okay," Dimase said. "I'm coming straight to the hospital. Meet me there. Who's in charge?"

"Me and the state police captain, but he's callin' the shots."

"Sheriff," Dimase said, "this is very important. We must look for anything that would provide a possible DNA sample of the killer. Please ask them to slow down and coordinate with us on that. It could be on a doorknob, a cup, the body of a victim, or anything. This is crucial. We must understand if this attacker is the same person who attacked the two Acadia LaFleurs."

"Attacked the two Acadia LaFleurs? Are you sure about that?"

"Yes, I didn't tell you yet because I just found out myself. We have conclusive DNA evidence that the same person attacked both Acadias."

"Is that right? I didn't know we had DNA evidence on the attack up here. Where'd that come from?"

"It's a long story. I'll explain it to you later, but trust me—we must find out if this is the same person coming back once again and if the other dead people in the hospital are tied in somehow. It seems impossible after all this that someone could randomly kill the patient next to Acadia and not have it connected in some way."

"But how?" Sheriff Roy exclaimed. "It don't make no sense. He tries to kill Acadia once, and then he don't touch her when he kills the guy next door and two members of the hospital staff?"

"Sheriff, have someone in your office find out as much as they can about the three new victims. What they did for work, hobbies, family—anything that might tie them to each other or to Acadia. My guess is you won't find anything. Maybe they were just in the wrong place at the wrong time. Maybe some of these deaths are just meant to cover up the true target—meant to confuse us."

"Well, they're doing a damn good job."

"I know. Look, focus on preserving any possible DNA opportunity, and get your guys working on the victim backgrounds. I'll see you in ninety minutes."

Dimase finished dressing, threw his travel bag into the back of the Ford rental, and set out for Cabrini Hospital in Alexandria. Once underway, he called Ben Johnson on his cell and filled him in on the latest events. Ben was incredulous but relieved that no further harm had come to Acadia.

"What are you thinking?" Ben asked Dimase.

"I hate to say it, Ben, but I think Acadia was the target. If the profiles on the three victims from last night come up as completely random and unrelated, then the only explanation that fits is that the guy was going back after Acadia to finish the job, and somehow, he got interrupted and had to escape. That is the simplest explanation. I suppose it's possible one of the three victims was the intended target for some completely unrelated reason and all the other stuff was designed to disguise that intention, but that is highly unlikely."

"That doesn't make sense to me either, so why are they after Acadia? I know her as well as anyone. I can't think of any reason why anyone would want to kill her," Ben said.

"We'll know more if we can get a DNA sample from the murders last night. I was going to call you today anyway. We got confirmation yesterday on a DNA match between the attacker in Alexandria and the attacker in Sugartown. It's definitely the same guy. The same guy who attacked your Acadia murdered the other Acadia in Sugartown two weeks later."

"Holy shit!" Ben exclaimed.

"Think about this, Ben. That evidence means it was, in all probability, a contract killing; the same guy went after two different, apparently unrelated people, and the only common denominator is that they share the same name."

"Who would order a contract killing, and why on both women?"

"I am starting to develop several theories," Dimase said. "I believe the attacks on both Acadias were an ordered hit. One was designed to disguise the true motive for killing the other target. One was camouflage, and the other was real."

"Which one do you think was the real target?" Ben asked.

"What about Alphonse?" Dimase asked in return. "Do you think he found out about you and Acadia? Could he have been motivated by jealousy or revenge?"

Ben was silent for a moment. "It's possible, I guess, but my gut tells me no. First, I don't think he knows. Second, I don't think he'd care that much if he did know, as long as he wasn't publicly embarrassed. He's been doing his own thing for years. Third, family is everything to him in his own weird way. If he ordered something like that, he'd be hurting his children terribly. He'd run the risk of losing them forever if it ever came out. Then there's the whole aspect of a political scandal if a guy gets caught ordering a hit on his own wife. I don't think it's him. He'd let sleeping dogs lie."

"I agree," said Dimase. "I have thought that all through as well, but I wanted to hear it from you first."

"What do you think?"

"I have developed other evidence to suggest that young Cady LaFleur was the intended victim of a contract hit. I believe she was the target, and your Acadia was attacked to throw everyone off track."

"So you think the only reason to attack my Acadia was to disguise and confuse?" Ben sounded dazed. "What about last night's attack at the hospital? What was that?"

"That was someone trying to finish the job, and fortunately, they got interrupted and had to make a quick exit."

"If that's true, Dimase, we've got to get Acadia out of there. They might come back and try again. If she was just meant to be a diversion and the hooker, Cady, is already dead, why go after my Acadia now?"

"If we are on the right track, I believe there is only one thing she could know that would have anything to do with a contract hit on young Cady. She saw her attacker, and if she wakes up, she can identify him."

"I have an idea," Ben said. "We have to move Acadia. Fischer, Forbes, and Johnson owns a high-end, state-of-the-art rehabilitation center as part of one of our senior living developments in Atlanta. We could move her there in secret and under a false name. No one will know she's there, except immediate family. I can put in all kinds of security and bring in any additional medical equipment or personnel they would need. I have control over the place if I want. It will be the safest thing."

"How will you get the family to go along with that?"

"I'll go to Francois in Washington. I'll give him a confidential update on the entire situation. I'll convince him of the danger. I've known him for forty years. He respects me. He'll listen to me. I'll influence him to prevail upon Alphonse. In the meantime, you do the same thing in Alexandria with Alphonse, Clement II, and Babette. They deserve to know what's going on. When they understand the severity of the situation and Francois is also on board, they will all agree."

"Okay," Dimase said. "It sounds like a plan. I'll take care of things on my end."

"Dimase, thank you, my friend. I don't know what I would have done without you. Please protect her until we can get her to safety."

CHAPTER 19

Washington, DC

The following day, Ben took an early flight to DC, and by ten o'clock, he walked into the reception area of Francois LaFleur's congressional office. He hadn't been there in years, but he knew he wouldn't have any problem in getting a last-minute appointment, for two reasons: first, Acadia was Francois's sister-in-law, and second, Francois owed him.

Ben intentionally had avoided going into any detail on the phone. He had to persuade Francois of the gravity of the situation and present his best argument up close and personal. The one sticky point Ben had to finesse was to explain his own involvement and why he was the person approaching Francois about Acadia's safety. He'd thought about that aspect on the plane and come up with a tentative plan.

A secretary showed Ben into the inner office, and Francois came from behind the desk to greet him warmly with a handshake and a hug. "Ben, my friend, it's good to see you. Please, sit down," Francois said, gesturing to a seating arrangement on one side of the room.

"It's good to see you too," Ben replied. "The years have been good to you." Francois was thicker and grayer but otherwise looked the same.

The two men sat across from each other in red leather-bound armchairs separated by an antique coffee table. Francois turned serious. "You said this is about Acadia?" He leaned back in his chair and raised his eyebrows.

Ben took a breath and hoped he sounded confident. "A good friend of mine, Dimase Augustin, is a former homicide detective and now does private investigation. He was working a related case that led him to look into the attack on your sister-in-law. As we speak, he is meeting with Alphonse, Clement II, and Babette back in Alexandria to bring them up to speed. He has uncovered some shocking developments. I will update you momentarily. He asked me to come to you because he knows I have a relationship with you and your family that goes back to the river walk project days and that I have access to all kinds of real estate facilities. Quite frankly, he hoped you have enough trust and respect for me to take seriously what I am about to tell you and to prevail upon Alphonse to take immediate action."

"Okay," Francois replied neutrally.

Ben tried to read Francois but couldn't tell if he was getting through or not. He started at the beginning and told Francois everything, starting with young Cady LaFleur, her diary entries, and her letters home to her mother. He talked about her work as an elite prostitute at the Premiere Escort Service and Dimase's theory about a senator with the nickname Dickie who had a place at the Watergate apartments. He covered the phone text that young Cady wasn't supposed to see and how she'd fled Washington to return to Louisiana. He explained in detail to Francois why they thought his sister-in-law had been attacked as a decoy and that two weeks later, young Cady LaFleur had been killed by the same man—a contract hit, they suspected.

Lastly, Ben went through the details of the triple homicide at Cabrini Hospital two nights earlier and told him they thought Acadia had been the target, due to the bad guys fearing she would awaken from her coma and identify her assailant; thus, the attackers were desperate to silence her and would stop at nothing.

Francois listened in stunned silence. "You are telling me that someone in Washington—perhaps some senator named

Dickie—ordered a hit on a hooker who saw something she shouldn't have, and at the same time, they went after my sister-in-law as a diversion simply because she had the same name?"

"Yes," Ben said. "That is exactly what I'm telling you. We also believe that Acadia is still in extreme danger. These people are ruthless and brutal. We think they might well come for her again. They may have nothing to lose. They may have access to significant manpower and resources. Francois, she must be moved for her own safety."

"I can see that," Francois said haltingly. "Of course she should be moved, but what do you want from me?"

"Nothing except to influence your brother to go along with our plan to protect Acadia. Detective Augustin is reviewing it with Alphonse and his children right now. I know your brother will do whatever you say. Augustin got me involved because he thought Fischer, Forbes, and Johnson might have a medical facility somewhere where we could move Miss Acadia. We do have such a place, Francois, in Atlanta. It is attached to a senior living development project, a state-of-the-art medical and rehabilitation facility. The detective proposes to move Miss Acadia there under a false name and a complete veil of secrecy. Only her most immediate family will know her whereabouts. We must hide her away until this situation passes. Do you understand?"

Francois looked distracted, as if his brain were working on three different things at once. Nonetheless, he agreed to move Acadia. "Of course, we must do everything possible to protect Miss Acadia. Thank you, and thanks to Detective Augustin for helping us out. I will call Alphonse at once."

"Good," Ben said. "I will coordinate the arrangements directly with Detective Augustin. Please convince Alphonse to authorize the move as soon as possible. We will take care of everything else." Ben wondered if Francois had any inkling of the true nature of his relationship with Acadia, but he could not be concerned with that now.

Ben excused himself, and the men said goodbye. He was relieved that Francois had gone along with the plan but anxious to touch base with Dimase and get going with the move. He didn't want Acadia to spend one more night in Cabrini Hospital. He also realized that the move would give him an excuse to see her. The new place was his facility, and he, along with Dimase, would now be pretty much in charge of everything, including timing, security, and medical personnel.

Ben was both relieved he could be with Acadia soon and afraid of what he would see. He already knew from Dimase how bad it would be, but he resolved to brace himself. Anything was better than being kept from her, especially in her darkest hour.

◆ ◆ ◆

After Ben left, Francois immediately began trying to track down his brother, Alphonse. Within minutes, he got a call back.

Alphonse was fuming. "What the fuck is going on?" he screamed into the phone. "This Dimase guy says they think a senator named Dickie with a place at the Watergate ordered a contract hit on my wife in order to cover up another hit on some hooker who happened to have the same name. Are you shittin' me? My wife! I'll kill that motherfucker. What the fuck, Francois? Why would he do that?"

"I don't know, little brother, but we're going to find out." Francois was pissed off too.

"We both know it's him. I thought he was our friend. There ain't no other senator named Richard with a place at the Watergate. The stupid fuck. He thinks he's going to be the leader of the free world or some shit, and he can't even keep his dick in his pants for five minutes. There ain't no other senator who would put out a hit on a hooker. It's him—the bastard—and what did this hooker see on his phone anyway? The stupid shit probably compromised the whole organization just because he needed a piece of ass, and then he brought my family into it. He hit my wife just to confuse everybody? My family, Francois!"

"I know, I know." Francois tried to calm his brother, even though he was equally angry and perplexed. "You need to get up here. Let me think. We'll figure out what to do next."

"Think?" Alphonse exploded. "I'm going to walk into that prick's office and tear him apart with my bare hands!"

"I know, Alphonse. I know. I want to do the same thing. No one does this to our family and gets away with it, but we have to be smart about it, and we have to find out why."

"Ain't gonna make no bit of difference why, Francois. He's a dead man. He ain't gonna lead shit."

"Alphonse, stop and think for a moment. This detective guy, Dimase or whatever his name is, and the authorities—it's only a matter of hours or a day or two at most before they figure out that Monroe is the senator they are looking for. He's the only senator who fits that profile. They are going to know it's him, and they are going to try to figure out what was in the text that started all this. It must have been something bad for Monroe to order a hit to take the hooker out."

"Yeah, that's all fine, but he went too far when he involved my family. This motherfucker is going down."

"I'm with you, Brother. All I'm saying is let's keep our cool. Let's not tip our hand right away. I'll set up a meeting with Monroe. We have to act like everything is normal, at least at first. Then we'll decide what to do next. Don't worry. I've got your back. No one fucks with the LaFleurs like this, not even Dick Monroe."

CHAPTER 20

Frank Harrington hurried down the steps at FBI headquarters and tried to look casual as he walked several blocks until he was safely away. Every car that slowed to make a turn stood out. Every person who tried to make eye contact unnerved him just a little more, and the people who didn't make eye contact unnerved him even more. Paranoia was starting to close in. He hailed a taxi and gave the guy directions. When he arrived at his destination, he paid the driver in cash and walked to a secluded area.

Monroe had seemed none too happy when Harrington had called him on the phone to arrange an emergency meeting.

Things were out of control in Alexandria, and Harrington had acted unilaterally to put an end to it. He'd put word down the chain to his bureau asset in Alexandria that the last link in the chain had to be severed immediately. The guy had gone off the rails and was calling all kinds of attention to the situation. If he hadn't fucked things up in the first place and gone after the wrong Acadia LaFleur, no one would have noticed a thing. Now, because of that idiot, they had four murders and one attempted murder at three different locations and all kinds of investigations going on.

The state police, two local sheriff's departments, and some detective from up north were all looking into the hospital murders and the situation with the two Acadia LaFleurs. The guy they were looking for wasn't FBI, just a low-level informer who'd been recruited to hit the hooker. How he'd fucked things up so much was beyond comprehension.

The risk of compromise was now too great. The guy was obviously panicked and acting irrationally. There might have been a minimal risk that the LaFleur woman would awaken from her coma and identify him, but that also might never have happened, and if it had, they probably could have managed the situation.

Now the idiot had been identified running around with a towel on his head, killing people in the hospital, and apparently thinking he was invisible or something. The state police had clear security footage of him parking his pickup truck in the garage and entering the hospital with a bouquet of flowers. Only on the way out, after he'd started killing people, had he tried to disguise himself with the towel. *Moron.*

Harrington had to question the judgment of the FBI handler who'd recruited the guy in the first place. The idea behind a secret chain of command loosely linking isolated cells was to provide maximum security for those at the top and plausible deniability between operatives in different cells who might be involved in different activities. Monroe's network, though relatively diverse and far reaching, was not exactly a shadow government, at least not yet. It was more like a secret society, informally recruited and put together through word of mouth and long-standing relationships. Many were career bureaucrats or government employees, while others, like Senator Monroe, were longtime politicians.

To become part of the secret alliance, one had to be recommended and vouched for by an existing member. There were no large meetings or formal interviews. The candidate's background was discreetly vetted, and his immediate sponsor might ask a few pointed questions and provide more clarification. The identities of other members of the organization would become apparent only if and when one had a specific need to interact with them. Individual cells were not generally aware of other cells' operations.

Money flowed surreptitiously throughout the organization. The goal was not to implement some political ideology in whose cause the members were passionately united. To the contrary, political backgrounds varied significantly. Instead, there was a more cynical motivation at play in the birth and expansion of the secret society. The common bond was plain and simple, something basic to the entire history of humankind. At its core, the alliance was about survival, money, and power.

From top to bottom, there was no loyalty to flag or country or sense of shared patriotism. To be in the network, the prime requisite was a shared view that the forces of history were reshaping the country. That was seen not as a good or bad thing but as merely an opportunity and something they had to stay out ahead of. As with secret societies from La Cosa Nostra to the Third Reich and others throughout history, the objective was to maintain power and control and continue as part of the ruling class.

Harrington saw Monroe's car pull into a space in the rest area off Interstate 95. It was a new meeting location, a last-minute choice that minimized the chance of being observed. Monroe climbed out of the backseat and walked to the edge of the picnic area, where he joined Harrington at an isolated table. "What the hell is going on down there, Frank? I see a triple homicide on the news and a manhunt for some guy named Rufus Manteau. Is that what I think it is? Does it have anything to do with us?"

"Yeah, it does," Harrington said, seeing no point in beating around the bush, "but it's contained. We're on top of it."

"What the hell happened?" Monroe asked again, his jaw clenched and his eyes narrowed.

"Manteau is local muscle that the guy in our office hired to do the hooker. He's the one who hit the wrong Acadia LaFleur before he did the hooker two weeks later. He went rogue. He panicked. We didn't tell him to do anything. He was afraid the old lady would come out of her coma and identify him. He took it upon himself to go back and finish her so that wouldn't happen."

"Well, we've got to make sure it doesn't happen now. Not with her—I'm talking about with Manteau. I don't want anything left of him for her to identify except a picture. That will end that, even if she does wake up."

"Already ordered," Harrington said, "but Manteau is on the run. We're not sure where he is, and with everyone looking for him, there's no telling who will find him first, us or the cops."

"That's just great," Monroe replied sarcastically. "This whole thing is going sideways. We have to move up the timetable on Operation SCOTUS. I want to go next week."

"Next week?" Harrington exclaimed. "I'm not sure we're ready yet. If we rush things, it increases the risk exponentially of something going wrong." He tried to ignore the slight tremor in his left hand. Monroe was completely off his rocker.

"Plenty's already gone wrong, Frank," Monroe said. "We can't afford to wait any longer. Once it's done, it's done. There'll be two openings on the court, and the balance will be changed. If a couple of our guys get caught up in it, that's a cost of doing business. As long as it doesn't get directly back to us. They can be suspicious all they want, but we can't allow anything to get tied to us. If there are any loose ends after the fact, cut them off. I want this done and done fast."

"What if the other guys get Manteau before we do?" Harrington asked. "He could give up his handler, who is a bureau guy."

"All the more reason to move quickly; we can't give them time to figure anything else out. What can this Manteau guy and his handler actually give up anyway? Think about it. Between the two of them, they know a hit was ordered on a hooker from Washington, DC, named Acadia LaFleur. They know the Acadia LaFleur in a coma was attacked in a case of mistaken identity. They don't know why the hit was ordered. They don't know who ordered it. I think we're okay, but we can't waste any more time."

Harrington was pensive. "Once they know the hit was ordered from DC, if they get to the handler, they'll leverage him all kinds of ways to move back up the chain."

"You're right," Monroe said. "That's why we've got to take preemptive action. You need to skip over a few links and go down there to take out the handler yourself. Even if they catch Manteau first, then it won't matter if he gives up the handler. If the guys in the FBI chain above the handler don't know why he was taken out, there's nothing for the feds or anyone else to leverage up the chain. It stops with your handler."

"You want me to personally take out my own guy? Are you serious?" Harrington asked.

"It's collateral damage, Frank. Do you see any other way? If you take care of that, we're in the clear from that end of the operation. The whole contract-hit-on-a-hooker part of the investigation will dead-end; it will go away. Then all we have to worry about is making sure things don't get screwed up next week on this end. I want Operation SCOTUS to go next week, and I want you to take care of your guy in Alexandria."

Harrington got up to leave, shoving his hands stiffly into his pockets. He hadn't signed up to be a hit man. It wasn't so much the killing that bothered him, although he didn't like having to do his own people and definitely didn't like the exposure of having to do it himself. Disloyalty was bad for business. After all, he was deputy assistant director of the fucking FBI, for God's sake! But more than anything, the source of his angst stemmed from his fear of getting caught. Monroe was getting reckless. The FBI was in the business of catching bad guys. The longer this went on, the greater the odds they would soon catch him. "All right, Senator," he said bitterly. "You're calling the shots. I just hope we're all still standing two weeks from now."

CHAPTER 21

As soon as Ben left his meeting with Francois and was back in the privacy of his limo, he hit the button to put up the dividing glass between himself and the driver and called Dimase to see how things had gone with Alphonse. "How'd it go?" Ben asked.

"He's really steamed," Dimase replied. "He's not the best at hiding his feelings. I think he may know more than he's letting on, but he's all on board with the move. He, Clement II, and Babette gave me carte blanche. They all want her out of here immediately."

"Good," Ben said. "I'm going to Atlanta this afternoon to make sure everything is ready on that end. They are expecting a comatose female patient to arrive within the next twenty-four hours. I've hired a team of medical specialists to oversee her care. Did you speak to Larson about the extra security?"

"Yes," Dimase replied. "That's all set. He's put in place rotating four-man teams. There will be two in uniform, and two will be undercover. Acadia will be on an isolated floor where you need a security code to get by the door. We've moved a couple people around to set it up that way on a temporary basis. There will be a uniform at the door to her room and a nurse and orderly undercover on her floor. There will be another uniform on the locked door to gain access to that wing of the floor. We've linked in to the facility's security cameras and supplemented that system with a couple extra cameras around the area of her room. We have a van outside monitoring the cameras as well as looking for any unusual arrivals in the parking lot. The regular security team for the building has been briefed, and they've added an extra uniform of their own in the lobby. Trust me, Ben; she will be better protected than if she were president of the United States."

"Good. Thank you, Dimase. Cost is not an issue here. I just want her to be safe. What is Alphonse going to do?"

"He said he's got to go back to Washington to meet with his brother, Francois. I suggested to him, Clement II, and Babette that they all stay away from Atlanta for a few days until we are more confident of the security situation. I wouldn't want them leading the bad guys right back to Acadia. They agreed to go about their normal activities for a few days as long as we keep them totally informed as to her health. They may arrange to travel separately and visit her sometime next week."

"Good," Ben said. "When will she leave?"

"My plan is to take her in the middle of the night. I have an ambulance coming at two o'clock in the morning, and then we will transport her by private air ambulance to Atlanta. She should arrive at your facility by five o'clock—as Susan Smith, a wealthy car crash victim from California."

"Thank you, my friend," Ben said. "You really came through for me once again." He shifted a little in his seat. "Why do you think Alphonse is in such a hurry to get back to DC?"

"I'm not sure, but his whole demeanor changed as I told him what had happened. He could barely contain his anger. He and Francois are pretty well connected in that town. I wonder if he has his own idea about who Senator Dickie might be and whether he's the one who ordered the hit."

"Interesting," Ben said. "Anything is possible. Any word yet from Larson on the short list of senators?"

"He's my next call. He's got people working on it. Our first focus was to get all this set up and take care of the security arrangements in Atlanta."

"Right. Let me know as soon as you hear anything," Ben said, and he hung up.

◆　◆　◆

Dimase had determined that he would personally remain at Cabrini Hospital with Acadia until she was safely en route later that evening. Sheriff Roy agreed to post extra security. The state police had already identified Rufus Manteau as the hospital assailant, and a massive manhunt was underway to locate him. It was unlikely he would return to the hospital, but Dimase was unsure whether anyone would come in his place. Clearly, somebody wanted to silence Acadia. Rufus Manteau was not operating on his own. Whoever had ordered the original hit was still out there.

Dimase's phone buzzed to alert him to a new text message. It was from Larson: "Short list is very short. Only eight senators with first name Richard or Dick. None have lease at Watergate, but is hard to tell with corporate names and probably fake names on tenant list. Will keep digging."

The text went on to list the full names of the eight senators and which states they represented. Dimase looked over all the names, but none in particular jumped out at him.

Dimase sent Larson a return text: "Good. Put a couple guys at Watergate. See if they can spot anyone on the list coming or going. After Acadia is moved, I'm headed to DC with Ben Johnson to see what we can figure out."

CHAPTER 22

When Alphonse arrived in Washington, he caught a cab from the airport and went directly to his brother's congressional office. Francois was expecting him, and the two of them retreated to his inner sanctum. Although it was not yet noon, Francois poured himself a Jim Beam straight up and one for Alphonse as well.

"When do we see Monroe?" Alphonse asked.

"I didn't call him," Francois responded. "I thought it would be better if we didn't give him any time to think on it in advance. I want to ask him straight up and out of the blue if he ordered a contract hit on Acadia. I want to see his reaction. I want to know if he's telling the truth. If he doesn't know the question is coming, we'll be able to tell."

"All right," Alphonse agreed reluctantly, "but if what Ben Johnson and his detective friend say is true, I may not kill him right then and there, but I will tell him I'm coming for him."

Francois took a sip from his drink. "I've been thinking on this a bit, Phonse. Something doesn't add up. It doesn't make sense for Monroe to do what they said—not at his level. He knows I'm one of his group. He knows you. What would he have to gain? Why would he want to piss me off? Maybe someone below him ordered it. Maybe somebody freelanced, and he didn't know about it."

"We won't know until we ask him. When do we see him?" Alphonse said.

"Let's see if we can track him down," Francois said. He called a cell number he had for Monroe, but there was no answer. He called Monroe's chief of staff, who said the senator was out on private business for the afternoon. Francois caught Alphonse's glare and pretended to be busy with his phone as he tried to think.

Francois had no specific detail with regard to who was doing what in Monroe's operation. Nonetheless, he was part of a small group of a dozen senators and congressmen who'd functioned as a think tank when the scheme was originally cooked up on a hypothetical basis over cocktails at an informal retreat. As a powerful twenty-year congressman with a multigenerational pedigree as a southern Democrat, Francois had been recruited to Monroe's secret society several years earlier. Operational detail, as always, was on a need-to-know basis. Monroe was the de facto leader of the group and the member with the most connections to the FBI and CIA.

Francois recalled that the overall concept had been enthusiastically discussed late into the evening, but after that, there had been no follow-up that involved him. When Justice Thompkins recently had passed away from natural causes, Francois immediately had recognized the scenario. Now he wondered if the reason for all the killing was something that some poor hooker accidentally had seen in a text on Monroe's phone. Francois decided to compose a text that would get Monroe's attention.

Francois typed out the text: "Urgent update. Operation SCOTUS. Must meet." He hit Send and put the phone on the desk.

Within two minutes, his phone pinged with a reply: "Francois?"

Francois simply replied, "Urgent. Now. Where?"

Again, a reply came back: "1 HR. WGate."

"K."

Francois looked at his brother. "Well, that got a reaction. He'll see us at his place at the Watergate in an hour."

An hour later, Francois's driver dropped him and Alphonse at the front entrance to the Watergate apartments. They passed by the security desk, where a message had been left for the guard to expect them and send them up. They took the elevator to Monroe's floor, and the senator was waiting at the open door to his suite, beckoning them inside. He appeared to be alone.

"I've been expecting to hear from you," he said before either of the brothers had a chance to speak. "There's been a terrible screwup, and I just learned of it myself. Alphonse, I am so very sorry for what happened to your wife. You must believe me. Have you seen the latest news from Alexandria?"

Without waiting for an answer, Monroe clicked on CNN. A news anchor provided detail as a rolling headline scrolled across the bottom of the screen: "FBI Agent Found Shot in Car." The anchor said, "To repeat, about one hour ago, we received the first reports of a breaking story out of Alexandria, Louisiana, where an unidentified FBI agent has reportedly been found shot to death in a parked car. The discovery was made just after eleven o'clock this morning on a dirt road off the main highway, about eight miles from the downtown area. Authorities have not yet released the agent's identity and refuse to speculate at this point as to motive. In a related story, the manhunt for thirty-five-year-old Rufus Manteau has now been expanded from Louisiana to include several surrounding states. Manteau is wanted in connection with the triple homicide that occurred two nights ago at Cabrini Hospital, also located in Alexandria. Authorities have refused comment as to whether the death of the FBI agent is in any way related to the Manteau investigation."

Monroe turned the TV off. "That's the man you want, Alphonse: Rufus Manteau. He's the one who decided to attack your wife. Him and only him, all by himself."

Alphonse still had not spoken a word.

Francois jumped in. "Why would he do that, and what does that have to do with the death of an FBI agent? Why are so many people dying in Alexandria, Dick? What the hell is going on? We have a right to know."

"We had a security breach. It involved a young hooker who went by the trade name Daisy May. She had to be addressed. No one knew her real name was Acadia LaFleur—at least I didn't know. We didn't even know she was from Louisiana; that all came out later."

"There is a detective investigating the attack on our Acadia and the murder of the other Acadia," Francois responded. "Did you know that your young hooker kept a diary, Dick, and that she wrote dozens of letters to her mother?"

Francois and Alphonse both watched Monroe's face carefully for any reaction.

"What's that got to do with me?" he asked.

"You tell us," Francois replied. "The authorities have all that stuff now. As we speak, they are looking for a senator who goes by the name Dickie and has a place at the Watergate. Know anybody who fits that profile, Dickie?" He watched as Monroe blanched and looked as if he were about to lose his lunch. "They came to us yesterday. Their theory is that this Senator Dickie ordered a contract hit on a hooker named Acadia LaFleur and that he also ordered a hit on Alphonse's wife simply to create a diversion. Is that true?"

"No, that's insane," Monroe replied. "Why would I ever do that? I told you: it's that fool Manteau. He is such an idiot that he attacked the wrong Acadia LaFleur. I'm sorry, Alphonse; it's true. He told his handler that he knew Acadia LaFleur and that he would take care of it. Then he attacked your wife. It was just one moron who didn't know what the fuck he was doing. That's why the hooker was killed two weeks later. He had to go back and fix it."

"Who's going to fix my wife?" Alphonse exploded.

Francois quickly stood in front of Alphonse and clamped his brother in a tight bear hug, waiting for him to calm down.

Monroe moved to the bar in an apparent attempt to defuse the situation. He pulled out glasses and ice, as if he were serving at a party.

"I know, I know. I'm sorry," Monroe said, practically whining, as he poured himself a scotch and motioned for the brothers to join him.

"Who was the handler?" Francois asked. "Is it the guy on the news, the FBI agent?"

"Yes," Monroe replied resignedly. "You said you had something urgent regarding Operation SCOTUS. What is it? How much do you know?"

"Only what I can guess," Francois said. "I figured you would take the operation live once I saw that Thompkins had passed away from natural causes. It's exactly the scenario we were all talking about. Other than that, I don't know anything, except to tell you that I think they are going to be looking at you for the hooker murder—real hard and real soon. What was in that text that got her killed, Dick? What did she see?"

"Thompkins's name was in the text. There was also a reference to Operation SCOTUS going green. I don't know if she even understood what she was looking at or not, but it was too much of a risk to let it go. Even if she didn't realize what it was about at the time, if she was ever questioned later, what she saw might provide corroborating evidence. She was a liability we couldn't afford."

"So that's it," Francois said. "All this craziness in Alexandria is because of one text—because you can't keep your dick in your pants? Jesus Christ, Dick. What are we—a bunch of novices? You've got to do better than that."

"You're right." Monroe kicked back his scotch and poured himself another. "I'm sorry, but we can't change what has already happened. Next week is the tipping point. We must successfully complete the mission. Once that is accomplished, we will be on our way to total control. If we get past next week, all the pieces will be in place. These amateurs running for office can spout their socialist platitudes all they want, but they have no idea how to run a government. We will be positioned to be a government within the government. We will pull the strings and control the money—the three of us and the others. There will be no one to even slow us down, let alone stop us."

Francois looked at his brother. Alphonse hadn't made a move toward Monroe's expensive scotch, but every pore of his being exuded fury. Francois recognized that no further purpose would be served by directing their ire toward Monroe, and he terminated their meeting.

On the way downstairs, he prevailed upon Alphonse to redirect his anger toward Manteau. There was too much at stake to approach the situation any other way. Sooner or later, Manteau would be picked up dead or alive, Francois pointed out. Sooner or later, it would be easy enough for Alphonse to extract his revenge. Between all their mutual connections, there was not a prison anywhere where Manteau could not be reached for a price. The issues of family pride and street justice had to be kept separate from the larger matter at hand. Manteau's day would come, but for now, it had to be put on the back burner.

◆　◆　◆

As the LaFleur brothers left the Watergate and returned to their waiting limousine, a random passerby near the building's entrance made a call on his cell. "Larson? Sullivan here. I haven't seen anyone come or go who matches any of the eight senators on the list, but I did see someone you might be interested in."

"Who?" Larson replied.

"Congressman LaFleur and his brother. They went in for about an hour and came back out a couple minutes ago. I'll see if I can go inside and flash some ID and money around; maybe someone will give up who they went to see."

CHAPTER
23

Atlanta, Georgia

B en was waiting when the ambulance carrying Acadia arrived at five o'clock in the morning. He planned to personally supervise getting her settled in the new facility. The security team was in place, and medical personnel were standing by. If anyone wondered why Ben was so personally involved, no one would bring it up. Ben was the boss. He owned the place.

Ben's initial explanation to employees and staff was that he was doing a personal favor for an old family friend who'd been in a terrible accident and whose family wanted her to recover in anonymity. The security people Bill Larson had put in place were professionals. Their only concern was that they had a job to do, and they were there to do it. Except for the attending physician, the medical staff were all indirectly Ben's employees.

Ben kept his composure as they wheeled Acadia's gurney into her new location in the secure wing. He had tried his best to prepare himself but could hardly breathe when he saw how thin and frail she was. Once she was in place in her room, the doctor checked her vitals, and the guard was posted outside her door. Ben lingered, realizing he was on the security feed, being monitored inside the van in the parking lot.

When he was alone, he pulled the privacy curtain and went to Acadia's side. She looked nothing like she had the last time he'd seen her. Tears streamed down Ben's face. He could not hold his emotions in check any longer. He cried for their future, and he cried for their past. He gently held her hand and touched her fingertips with his own. Hope flooded through him. He didn't imagine it: the light sensation of an electrical connection still passed between them. Despite his pain, he smiled through the tears and kissed the tops of her fingers. Her beautifully manicured nails were starting to chip and fade. Tomorrow he would arrange for a manicurist to come in to fix her nails—something for both Acadia and him to hold on to, he hoped.

Ben returned to the private office he'd set up for himself in the executive suite on the top floor of the building. That would be his temporary headquarters for as long as necessary. He busied himself, tending to various business matters for the rest of the afternoon. At four o'clock, he had a scheduled FaceTime call with Dimase Augustin.

"Acadia is here," Ben said. "Everything went smoothly. I knew it would be bad, Dimase, but it wasn't real until I saw her."

"We must pray for a miracle," Dimase said. "They do happen."

"I hope you are right, my friend. I sincerely hope you are right. I want the people responsible for this. I want them now more than ever. Have you found anything yet on this Senator Dickie? Do you know who he is?"

"I think we do," Dimase said. "Something unexpected has occurred. I'm not sure what to make of it. I want your take."

"What have you got?" Ben asked, hoping for any kind of breakthrough that might lead them to the truth.

"We have people stationed at the Watergate, armed with photos of the eight senators on the short list. We've also reviewed all public listings of tenants. If one of those senators has a place there, it's not under his own name. One of our guys did see a pair of visitors who surprised him, and he called it in to Larson. Ben, it was Francois and

Alphonse. They arrived late morning, stayed about an hour, and left in the same limo they arrived in."

"What in the heck were they doing there? I wonder," Ben said. "Any idea who they visited?"

"Our guy went in and tried to ask around. He showed ID, tried to pass himself off as some kind of government investigator, and even tried to offer money to the guy at the desk, but he didn't get any bites. I guess the tenants there place a high value on their security and privacy. The employees weren't about to give anyone up."

"There must be some way to find out what they were doing there," Ben said. "Maybe we should just ask them."

"Maybe," Dimase said, "but I think we should hold off. About an hour after the LaFleur brothers left, we got a match on one of the short-list senators. Somebody else left the Watergate, and my guy recognized him from the photos. He took a couple pictures with his cell phone. The guy fits. It was Senator Richard Monroe from Illinois."

"Monroe!" Ben exclaimed. "I just had lunch with him last week. The chair of the Senate Finance Committee. I'm supposed to schedule a follow-up meeting with him in the next few days. Do you think Francois and Alphonse went to see him?"

"I can't prove it," Dimase replied, "but it seems like a reasonable possibility. I've got Larson running more background on Monroe. I'd like to know if there's anyone out there who ever heard him referenced by the nickname Dickie."

"Let's assume for a minute that Monroe is our guy and that Francois and Alphonse went to see him," Ben said. "That would mean Francois and Alphonse know more than they are telling us. It does seem to be odd timing that as soon as you and I debriefed the brothers on the text and told them we were looking for a senator at the Watergate called Dickie, Alphonse came back to Washington right away, and they both went running over to the Watergate. If Monroe is the senator at the Watergate whose text the hooker saw and who ordered the hit on her, are we still thinking he also ordered the hit on my Acadia as a diversion? It wouldn't seem to make sense if he's tied in with Francois and Alphonse somehow."

"Maybe they are not tied in," Dimase said. "Maybe the LaFleur boys recognized who we were talking about, and they went to confront him."

"I guess that's possible," Ben said. "What do you think we should do?"

"Let's give Francois and Alphonse some rope and let things play out a bit. Maybe they'll come to us with their suspicions and tell us about this meeting with Monroe. After all, we are supposed to be on the same side, are we not? I think we should proceed as if Monroe is our man. We will put him under surveillance and develop a strategy for the next step as we see more of what's going on."

"All due respect, Dimase, shouldn't we alert the FBI? They could probably tap his phone and put a lot more resources into background and surveillance than you and Larson can muster."

"There is only one problem with that," Dimase said.

"What?" Ben asked.

"Did you see the news out of Alexandria today about the dead FBI agent?"

"What?" Ben was surprised. "No, I haven't looked at the news all day. After I finished with Acadia, I went to my office and have been working on a corporate strategic planning document all afternoon. What happened?"

"An FBI agent out of the Alexandria field office was found shot dead in his car this morning—no motive, no suspect. Do you think it is a coincidence with everything else that's going on down there?"

"Holy shit!" Ben could not help himself. "It can't be coincidence, right?"

"No, I don't think so. I think it means the FBI is compromised. We have to be very careful, Ben. Something is going on here that is larger than the murder of some random hooker or, for that matter, the attack on Acadia. Think about what we do know. We're looking for Dickie at the Watergate. Monroe was at the Watergate today. And so were the LaFleur brothers. A multistate manhunt is on for some thug named Rufus Manteau. Manteau is wanted for the triple homicide at Cabrini Hospital. You and I believe he is also the same person responsible for the attacks on both Acadias. Do you think he just woke up one day and decided to do this on his own? No, he was ordered to carry out the attacks on Cady and Acadia. We think that order came from Monroe. How did the order get passed to Rufus Manteau, a local hoodlum and bartender?"

"I don't know," Ben replied.

"He needed a connection, because Monroe wouldn't do it himself. I believe it was from the dead FBI agent," Dimase said. "It fits. I believe he was the handler for Rufus Manteau. Now he's dead, and no one can link any of those murders to anyone higher up at the FBI or anyplace else higher up the food chain."

"Holy shit," Ben said once again.

"Yes, my friend, we are in dangerous territory indeed. Whatever is really going on here, I believe we are dealing with a conspiracy of the highest order."

CHAPTER
24

Dimase thought about the chart on the wall back at headquarters; Larson had filled him in, and pieces began coming together quickly. Within forty-eight hours, Larson and his team had done enough research to confirm that Senator Richard Monroe was indeed their man. They developed a large tree chart and started filling in the names of anyone associated with Monroe on different limbs and branches. They did their best to prioritize and categorize relationships by degree of depth, longevity, purpose, and frequency of contact. As different individuals were added, they in turn were subjected to vigorous background checks. Eventually, a picture began to emerge of Monroe's inner circle.

Once Monroe was identified at the Watergate, Larson and Dimase kept people on him 24-7. After they determined which unit Monroe was in, they matched it up against a tenant list and found that the lease was under a corporate name: RBM Holdings Inc. The *RBM* stood for Richard Bennett Monroe, a.k.a. Dickie. A team planted button cameras outside his apartment, and it wouldn't be long before there were listening devices inside and on his phone.

Trying to figure out what Monroe was up to proved somewhat more difficult than simply identifying him as the senator from Cady LaFleur's letters and diary. Monroe moved around a lot, and he hardly had used the Watergate apartment at all during the time they had been keeping tabs on him. After each day, he returned to his Georgetown residence, not the Watergate. The phone tap proved to be useless, as there had been no calls, either incoming or outgoing, thus far.

Over the next few days, Dimase's operatives tailed Monroe, tracking his contacts and adding them to the tree chart. They could not overhear any conversations, as meetings were held behind closed doors, and his cell phone was not tapped. Given Dimase's concern about corruption within the FBI, it was out of the question to ask for their assistance on anything directly involving Monroe.

Dimase was confident they were on the right track with Monroe, but he was still in the dark as to what the wider conspiracy might have been. He kept going over Cady's diary entry about the text on Dickie's phone: "something about some guy dying and some operation on his scotis, whatever that is."

"Who died?" Dimase said to himself out loud as he shaved in the bathroom of his DC hotel room. "What kind of operation did they have, and what did it have to do with Monroe?" He rinsed his face and toweled off. He then opened his laptop, signed in to the hotel Wi-Fi, and googled "What is your scotis?" Immediately, the screen populated with numerous items related to the Supreme Court.

Dimase slapped his forehead. "Of course! It's an acronym."

Why hadn't he seen it before? It had been right in front of him the entire time. The way Cady had referenced the word, he'd thought it was a body part or a medical term of some sort. Cady had written it all in lower case, not in caps, as an acronym normally would have been presented. She also had misspelled the acronym, substituting an *i* for the *u*. Dimase had been focused so intently on the physical clues and the rapid pace of events that he had glossed over that aspect of the text.

Dimase scrolled down the page, looking at different links.

"POTUS Set to Battle over SCOTUS"
"SCOTUS Balance to Change"
"SCOTUS to Operate Shorthanded"
"SCOTUS Fight Looms"

Several headings down, he read, "SCOTUS Justice Charles Thompkins Dead of Natural Causes at 86."

Dimase read through the article and several others related to Justice Thompkins's death. He was aware that Justice Thompkins had passed away a few weeks ago, but he hadn't thought much about it. There had been an autopsy and investigation, and by all accounts, the consensus was that he had simply died of old age. Was it possible there was more to the story? What the hell had Cady meant by "an operation on his scotis"? Had she been referring to Thompkins when she'd said someone had died? Had Monroe had something to do with Thompkins's death?

Cady must have seen something in the text serious enough to get her killed, but what? Was it possible Monroe had had Thompkins killed and gotten away with it? That seemed too far-fetched. After all, unless the entire autopsy process had been corrupted, everyone had agreed the justice had died of natural causes, and all had moved on.

Both sides of the political aisle had had full participation in the Thompkins autopsy and final report. The conservatives would never have signed off if they'd thought there was any hint of foul play. There was no way Thompkins could have been murdered. The cause of death was not an issue with anyone, and now the focus was entirely on who would replace him. *So what was it, Cady LaFleur? What was it that got you killed?*

Dimase had an idea. He hit speed-dial and got Ben Johnson on the phone. "Ben, I just realized something that I totally missed the first time around. I've been thinking about Cady LaFleur's diary entry about the text on Dickie's phone. We all believe it was that text that got her killed. We are also virtually certain at this point that Senator Monroe is the Dickie she was referring to in the text. What I didn't see until now was what she meant by an operation on the guy's 'scotis.' We were focused on other stuff and thinking that she was using slang to refer to a body part the dead guy had had an operation on. She didn't name who died, but I think she was talking about Justice Thompkins, and I think *scotis* is actually an acronym for 'Supreme Court of the

United States.' She misspelled it. Her text has something to do with Thompkins's death. I'm sure of it."

"Maybe, but I've met Thompkins before. Everyone knows he died of natural causes. There's no controversy about that, so what about it would have made Monroe order a hit on her?"

"I don't know. That's the part I can't figure out, but it must have something to do with the Supreme Court."

"Is there anything new on Monroe?" Ben asked.

"Not really," Dimase replied. "We're trailing him as best we can, building a name tree of everyone he comes in contact with and trying to vet those people and fill in the gaps as we expand the tree. The longer we continue, the better idea we'll get of who he's involved with. If there is some sort of conspiracy going on, we're bound to get at least a partial idea of who else might be involved, but it will take time."

"So where do we go from here?"

"I have an idea on how we might flush Monroe out. It could be dangerous, but if we're careful, it might work. It involves you."

"How so?"

"You said you are supposed to have a follow-up meeting with Monroe in the next few days. Why don't you go ahead and schedule that meeting as soon as you can?"

"Okay, what's the dangerous part?"

"What if we hit Monroe right between the eyes and catch him off guard? We know the text had something to do with Thompkins's death and with SCOTUS; we just don't know what. How about partway through the meeting, you look him in the eye and say, 'Dick, I know about SCOTUS,' and see how he reacts. You're good at reading people, and you're quick on your feet. Ad lib after that, and see what you can find out. It's also possible we might spook him, and he'll give something away after the meeting while we are still watching him."

"Sounds like it's worth a try," Ben said. "It will be interesting to see how he responds. He'll probably either try to recruit me or kill me; I don't know which."

"I agree it is dangerous, particularly for you. He's not going to try to kill you right there in the restaurant, but we'll definitely have to put in additional security measures for you after the fact."

"I'm game," Ben said. "I want this guy, and I want to know what the hell he's up to. Let's do it."

CHAPTER 25

Monroe turned around and faced front. There was nothing out of the ordinary behind him. Or was there? He caught himself constantly straining from the backseat to check the side-view mirrors for a tail. He saw nothing. But he could feel it; he was being watched. He now realized the authorities might be closing in on him as a person of interest relative to the Cady LaFleur murder. There had been many screwups, and with zero hour next week, it was imperative that he keep his thumb on Harrington.

Monroe had run the calculus through his head many times. Any evidence against him at that point was purely circumstantial. It might get uncomfortable for a while if he were sucked into any investigation, but if he stood his ground, eventually, the heat would pass, and he would be positioned where he wanted to be.

He'd seen it many times during his years in Washington. Regardless of any speculation or accusations against him, the formula was to delay, deny, and obfuscate. Evidence could be destroyed or lost. Memories, both his own and other persons', could suddenly become hazy. If worse came to worse, he would just run out the clock, and over time, any inquiry would simply become inconclusive and go away.

No one would ever see the actual text Cady LaFleur had seen. That phone, and all texts on it, had long since been destroyed. Whatever

Cady LaFleur had written in her diary or letters would be purely speculative, and there was no corroborating evidence. She hadn't known anything specific. The imagined fantasy from a dead hooker's diary, if it ever came out at all, would not be enough to bring down a sitting US senator, least of all him.

The bigger threat to Monroe was if something went wrong next week. The mess in Alexandria was contained now. Sooner or later, the authorities would catch Manteau, but there was no one else for Manteau to give up now that his local handler was dead; any investigation would dead-end right in Alexandria. People could speculate all they wanted about who might have killed the agent, but no one would actually know anything about it, and it was highly unlikely that investigators would skip up several links in the chain and tie it to Harrington back in Washington, DC.

Still, if Manteau were caught, it might be a nice twist and kill two birds with one stone if they gave Manteau up to Alphonse. Alphonse was looking for revenge. If Manteau was in prison, they could point Alphonse in the right direction and step back while that situation played out on its own. If Alphonse put a prison hit out on Manteau, not only would he get his revenge, but Manteau's death would deep-six any investigation stemming from the Alexandria field office of the FBI, and Monroe would have nothing to do with the hit on Manteau.

Monroe glanced in the mirror again. He directed his driver to make a series of evasive turns and direction changes. If he was being followed, he wanted to make sure they couldn't keep up. The focus now had to be exclusively on next week. Anything else was just noise and had to be put aside. Monroe had his faults and weaknesses, but he was resolute. He hadn't gotten to his current position without a willingness to take chances and a steadfast pursuit of his goals.

The senator was anxious to meet with Harrington now that the assistant deputy director of the FBI was back from his errand down south. It was obvious Harrington was not happy about having to personally take out the FBI agent in Alexandria. Monroe had to make sure Harrington put that behind him and got his head back in the game. Next week was crunch time. Harrington was also skittish about moving up the timetable on Operation SCOTUS. Monroe hoped the guy had the balls to pull it off and then play hardball through any possible aftermath.

Monroe and Harrington had gravitated to a two-tier system for communicating with each other. They were both well aware of the potential for phone conversations to be captured in real time, so they avoided phone calls completely. Instead, they used vague texts with coded references to set up clandestine face-to-face meetings. The texts were not likely to be intercepted and could be immediately deleted. Moreover, they could periodically destroy and discard the burner phones as a further precaution. After they set up a meeting via text, all conversation regarding Operation SCOTUS was direct and in person.

Monroe decided they should no longer meet at Arlington National Cemetery. It made good operational sense to move things around. He hoped Harrington was being equally as careful.

Monroe spoke again to his driver and, satisfied that no one had followed, got out at the front entrance to the Hamilton Hotel on Fourteenth Street. He walked briskly through the lobby and straight out the back door. Wearing a pair of sunglasses, he sauntered casually for two blocks to Sixteenth Street and ducked into a small bar called Off the Record.

Harrington was waiting, as expected, in a private booth in the back. He was not in a festive mood. They skipped salutations. Monroe said, "I see from the news that your trip was a success. Any issues?"

"No," Harrington replied.

"Good. Put it behind you. I want to know more about next week. Are you ready to go?"

"I thought you didn't want to know operational details."

"I would have preferred it that way, but there have been too many screwups, and there's too much at stake. How are you going to do it?"

"Succinylcholine."

"What's succinylcholine?"

"It's a drug used in surgical procedures. An overdose will make it look like a heart attack. It dissolves. It's untraceable."

"I like the idea," Monroe said. "But we originally said no poison. Are you sure it's untraceable?"

"Positive. The CIA has used it for years. The Russians use it as well."

"How would you administer it?"

"Ideally, a pinprick of an injection on the back of the tongue; that way, the injection site would never show up on autopsy."

"Very ingenious, Frank," Monroe said. "Just an unfortunate heart attack—untraceable. I like it. I hadn't thought it would be possible to do such a thing without leaving some evidence—some chemical trail or perhaps a mark on the skin. You are sure of all this?"

"Yes."

"When?"

"Next Tuesday. Sumner goes for an early morning jog. We looked for someplace on the route where we could ambush him, but there's nothing suitable. We think the best thing is to intercept him when he returns to his house and gain entrance with him. We'll have two guys dressed up like UPS guys. We'll leave a UPS truck parked in the street. They'll time it to walk up right as he's by his front door, and they'll force him inside. My guys are well trained. One of them will apply a sleep hold over the carotid artery. Once he's out, they will open his mouth and administer the injection. It will look as though he had a heart attack after his run."

"What could go wrong?" Monroe asked.

"Shit, Dick, something can always go wrong. Something you don't plan for, something unexpected. That's why I wish we weren't rushing the timetable. We've had to move everything up. This was the best scenario we could figure. What could go wrong? I don't know. I suppose if he can resist before we get the sleep hold on him, we might leave a mark or bruise on him somewhere if we are trying to subdue him. I'd say that's the greatest risk, but there's always a wildcard. Someone might see the guys entering the house with him. He could have an unexpected houseguest. Who knows, Dick? It should go off as planned, but anything could happen. That's why I hate rushing. It leads to mistakes."

"Okay, Frank. I get it," Monroe said. "The plan is good. The risk is minimal. We have to go sometime. We're going next week. Get your mind set, Frank. Put your game face on, and make it happen—one hundred percent commitment. There can be no looking back. Do you understand?"

"Yes," Harrington said sourly. "I get it."

"Will there be anyone else in the house?"

"We don't think so. His kids are in private school, and his wife has been away visiting her mother. We don't know when she's coming back. That's another risk, but we'll just have to adjust and manage it if she shows up."

"If she's there, you'll have to abort and go back another time, unless you can pull it off without her knowing or seeing anything."

"Right."

"What about security? What does he have?"

"There's Secret Service—same as all the justices. They don't live with him. They pick him up and bring him to work in the morning and drop him off if he's coming home. They escort him pretty much everywhere he goes—functions, dinners, and such. That's another reason we think the house scenario is the best approach."

"What about his morning run? Why don't they go with him on that?"

"We're not sure, but his pattern is to go alone. We've never seen anyone with him so far. We figure that's just something he added to his daily routine on his own. He probably doesn't tell them about it."

"Okay, we're at the five-yard line," Monroe said. "Let's punch it in."

CHAPTER 26

Monroe left the bar and hurried down the street, keeping his head down. It was noon, and Fiola, an upscale Italian restaurant on Pennsylvania Avenue, was just ahead. When Johnson first had called to set up another meeting, Monroe had hesitated, but when Johnson had dangled the prospect of getting the ball rolling on their relationship, the offer had been too much to resist. He knew Fischer, Forbes, and Johnson was about to close a deal for one of the largest reconstruction projects Manhattan had ever seen. Monroe wanted in.

He originally had pegged Johnson as a straight arrow, but now he was not so sure. If he could control Johnson and position his firm as a primary government contractor, it could mean hundreds of millions or even billions of dollars for Monroe and his people. Handled properly, Johnson's minority-owned firm could be pushed to the front of the line for dozens of massive federally funded projects over the next two decades. If Johnson was willing to play ball, the arrangement would be a virtual money-printing machine for all involved. Literally, the government would print the money; the senator and his cronies would steer the projects to Fischer, Forbes, and Johnson; and 10 or 20 percent would be laundered right back to Monroe and his associates.

When developed to its full potential, there would be rivers of cash flowing into dummy corporations, foundations, and offshore accounts.

For Monroe, any arrangement with Ben Johnson would be only one of many that he envisioned for his shadow government. When they pulled the strings for all three branches, the US government would become the most massive criminal enterprise in the history of humankind, and sitting at the top would be Dick Monroe.

If Operation SCOTUS was successful, the long-term plan was to find a path for Monroe to the presidency. That was the ultimate goal. They would first control the puppets and then eventually replace the puppets. Monroe's installation in the executive office was the holy grail. He would will it to happen. Over time, opposition would be strategically eliminated. He would have access to an unlimited reservoir of political cash. He would control the shadow government. From that point, it would be relatively easy to influence public opinion and either buy off or overwhelm competition or, in some cases, just make them go away.

The final phase of Monroe's grandest aspirations would be to emerge from the shadows and become the actual government. With the Supreme Court in his pocket and the power of executive orders and executive privilege at his command, with key supporters controlling every major congressional committee, Monroe could rule like a king. The people would not revolt. He would keep them pacified and mollified. He would implement a Grand New Deal. He would be FDR on steroids, orchestrating a basic level of cradle-to-grave security for all. Monroe would take care of his masses, and he would operate with impunity, reigning from on high, with both the carrot and the stick at his command.

After a few years, he would get the Supreme Court to go along with removing term limits and, as a practical matter, become president for life. To achieve greatness, one had to think big. He had to dream. That same scenario had played out in many other countries around the world and throughout history. Why not there in the United States? Why not with him? Time had a way of changing everything. The situation was ripe.

Each time Monroe capitalized on an opportunity in his life, it opened up new opportunities. He hadn't originally set out to be a god on earth, but from where he sat now, what was to stop him? Why not? He was singularly positioned at a unique point in history. Many of the most powerful leaders in history had emerged from poverty and insignificance to exert their will on the world. Adolf Hitler had been a house painter. Mao had been a peasant. Stalin had been born to a poor washerwoman. They, and others like them, had gone on to control hundreds of millions of people and rule large regions of the earth. Monroe had studied them all. They all had been ruthless, a common denominator Monroe was more than willing to share with them. All had followed a similar pattern: first control the mechanisms of government, then give the people what they want, and then control the people.

No one believed that could ever happen in the United States, but now Monroe not only could see it but would do it. All great empires throughout history had a life cycle. Why would the United States be any different? The push among young people for socialism was unprecedented. The opportunity to control another twenty million votes through offering a fast track to citizenship for the undocumented was also unprecedented. It was a one-time opportunity presenting itself at the perfect time for Monroe's purposes. Providing citizenship for that group would buy him at least two generations of loyalty and a free pass on most any other issue.

The opportunity was there to take the whole ball of wax. If Richard Monroe did not do it, then who would? If not now, then when? All the stars had aligned. It was all there for the taking. Senator Richard Monroe believed history had put him in that place at that time to do exactly that. It was his fate and his destiny to change the world—to fundamentally transform the most powerful nation on earth and walk among the giants of history.

The doorman held the door open for Senator Monroe as he walked into the restaurant, and the maître d' immediately guided him to the private room that had been reserved for lunch.

CHAPTER 27

Ben arrived at Fiola and was escorted to the small private room reserved for the meeting. Monroe had already arrived and was seated alone at one end of a long wooden table, waiting for him. Ben sat opposite and waited for the waiter to clear the room and close the door. Ben was wired for sound, and Dimase was parked in a van two blocks away, monitoring and recording the conversation.

Monroe spoke first to break the ice. "Ben, you indicated on the phone that you might be open to a broader relationship between the two of us. How would you see that playing out?"

Ben turned on his trademark charm and replied with an enigmatic smile, followed by silence. After a long, almost uncomfortable pause, he replied, "I know you have a grand vision for the country. So do I. Maybe we have common ground. Maybe we can help each other. You tell me what you see for the future, and I'll tell you whether we see it the same way or not."

"Very well. I see emotion overriding history," Monroe said, keeping the conversation on general terms. "I see an electorate hungry for change without really understanding what they are asking for. The traditionalists of the older generations are dying out and becoming outnumbered. The new electorate want a bigger government. They want the government to do more things for them. That means their loyalty can be bought. It's an opportunity, Ben. It's an opportunity for older, wiser heads like you and me."

Two waiters came back into the room, poured water, and took drink orders. After they left, Ben asked, "What kind of opportunity? An opportunity to do what?"

"A business opportunity, Ben—the largest, most massive business opportunity you've ever contemplated. Everything is lined up perfectly. Of course, we'll give the people what they want. The socialist wave is coming. It's already here. You and I both know that. There are too many people who want more of what they perceive other people to have. They are no longer satisfied with equality of opportunity; they want equal outcomes. They want to take from those who have too much and give it to those who have too little. You can see the appeal of it, can't you, Ben?"

Ben nodded in agreement. "The mood of the country has changed, Senator. There is little doubt about that. Some lessons of history have been forgotten. I agree with you that there is an insidious thread running through academia and the media, espousing that the United States has been more of a force for evil than for good—that we are all citizens of the world first, and that is where our allegiance should lie."

"Exactly," Monroe replied with enthusiasm. "I knew you were someone who would understand what is happening. So if all this is true, Ben Johnson, what do you do about it? What do you do for your firm? How do you survive if the overwhelming majority of the populace want to take from people like you and me and redistribute wealth among the masses in some futile attempt to create equality?"

Ben turned serious and looked Monroe directly in the eye. "You control the mechanisms of delivery. You stay above the fray. You give the people what they want, but gradually, you tighten control to the point where it can never be taken away."

Monroe seemed practically orgasmic. "Precisely!" he shouted. "I knew you got it. Every government in history has had ruling elite. There are no exceptions. The rules do not apply to them. The ruling elite make the rules; they don't follow them. You give the people what they want: more equal outcomes. You give them free education, but you control the message of that education. You provide a basic income for all, whether they work or not. You provide free health care. You provide government jobs to supplement the free marketplace, and you tax the hell out of everyone in return for all the free stuff. You control the media. You dictate the message. You discredit and weed out any malcontents."

"How does this apply to me?"

"Ben, you and I are businessmen at heart. I have a few gold coins in my pocket, and I am offering one of them to you."

"Are you recruiting me?"

"Would that be a bad thing?" Monroe said.

"It depends on what you are recruiting me for."

"I have many relationships at all levels throughout government and the private sector. Each and every one of those relationships is like-minded in terms of what is happening to the country. The momentum for change is too strong to resist. We may or may not like it, but we can't reverse it, so we must ride it out. We must adapt. We must survive. Do you see? The puppets who spout idealistic platitudes have no idea how to run a government. They are idealists, dreaming of some utopian vision. We have people in place who can run the day-to-day operation of the government. Then, if we play our cards right, we will become the government. We will be the ruling elite. We will take care of the people. The average standard of living will come down for many, but the basics will be provided for all. The majority will rule, and we will be exempt because we will be running all of it. Once we solidify our grasp, we will control the most powerful country in the history of the world. We will control policy. We will control the military, and most importantly of all, we will control the treasury. I am offering you one of those gold coins, Ben. I am offering you a chance to be one of us, the ruling class, a virtual god on earth, with more power and more wealth at your fingertips than has ever come before us."

Ben took a sip of his water. He couldn't believe the hubris of the guy. "What would you expect of me?"

"The Manhattan development project you alluded to on the phone is a good example, but it is a pittance compared to what we are talking about. You already have that project, so you don't really need us unless we can help with permitting or any other hang-ups like that. However, your offer of a consultancy is seen as a gesture of good faith, one that is much appreciated and could be easily duplicated. As we discussed last week, there is going to be a twenty-year flood of federal money going into infrastructure projects. We will control who gets those projects. Your Manhattan development you just closed on, big as it is, is chicken feed compared to what's coming. We will control the treasury of the US government. You and your firm can be the primary government contractor on dozens—even hundreds—of those projects. We're talking billions and billions of dollars, and that is only part of it. Ben, if you are one of us, there are countless other opportunities we all will participate in. Military contracts, space exploration, health care, pharmaceuticals—you name it. There will be endless opportunity for us all around the globe. We will be global elites. We will be the elite of all the elites."

Ben decided the time was right to strike. He wasn't sure if Monroe was some sort of evil genius or as mad as a hatter, but the man was at peak frenzy—a good time to take him down a peg. "What you are proposing requires a great deal of trust. Not everyone would see it the way we do. Some would call what you describe a conspiracy. If we aren't careful, we could all wind up in jail. There is more to me than meets the eye, Senator. I didn't get to where I am today without having networks and resources of my own. What you propose is interesting, but maybe it is I who should be recruiting you."

Monroe blinked in surprise. "What do you mean?"

"I mean that I've been building relationships in this town a lot longer than you have, Senator—this town and a lot of other towns and cities across the country for over forty years. Perhaps it is you and your people who should be joining me."

"I didn't realize ... I mean, I knew you were well connected, but I didn't think we might have so much in common. Are you actually organized?"

"To a degree," Ben replied evasively. "It's loose but effective. People are there when I need them. How about you?"

"It's similar." Monroe leaned forward. "Perhaps we should have an informal alliance flowing through the two of us for starters. If nothing else, such an arrangement would expand the reach of our mutual resources. It could be convenient and complementary from time to time while we wait for other pieces to fall into place."

"What other pieces?" Ben asked. He hoped Dimase was getting all the conversation back in the van.

"Pieces that will allow us to control more of the government. Today we are still in the shadows. Someday soon we will control all three branches of the government. When that happens, it will set the stage for us to step out of the shadows."

"What you say is possible," Ben said, playing along. "If you should know anything about me, you should know that I always do my research. I always know my partners, and I always know my opponents. I never engage in any business relationship on a blind basis. You should not underestimate me, Senator."

Monroe seemed to do his best to look innocent. "How would I underestimate you?" His face was blank, except for the twitch near his eyebrow.

"Dick," Ben said, leaning in, "I know about SCOTUS."

Monroe looked momentarily shocked but quickly recovered. "SCOTUS?"

"I know you are up to your ears in SCOTUS. I also know the feds are closing in on you for ordering the murder of a hooker in Louisiana. I know about the hit on the FBI agent in Alexandria. I know about Rufus Manteau, the guy on the run for the hospital murders. I know he was the guy who hit the hooker, and he also hit the other Acadia, Alphonse's wife. What the hell was up with that, Dick? I know all about the text on your phone the hooker saw that started this whole mess. You see, Dick, I have a lot of sources. I know a lot of things. That is what I mean when I say you should not underestimate me."

Monroe was speechless.

Ben pressed his advantage. "Who is it, Dick? Tell me who it is."

"Who?" Monroe stammered. "Who is who?"

153

"SCOTUS!" Ben shouted. "I want to know who and when. If you want to be partners with me, there are no secrets, Dick. Amateur hour is over."

"I can't tell you that," Monroe said softly. "It's on a need-to-know basis."

"Very well. Have it your way, but don't ask me to be partners with you if you don't think I have a need to know."

"It's for your own protection," Monroe said. "Don't you understand that?"

Ben shrugged. "But you know, don't you, Senator?"

"Look," Monroe said, "you seem to know a lot of things. I don't know how. I don't know who you've been talking to or who your sources are, but I give you credit. You must be as connected and omnipresent as you say. If you don't know who the target is, I'm not going to tell you. You are safer that way, and so am I. My not telling you is a way to prove my offer of friendship and loyalty. I will not tell you who, but as a gesture of good faith, I will tell you when. The timetable is next week. You will know when you see it on the news. That is the best I can do for you, Ben."

"What about the other shit headed your way?" Ben asked. "How do you plan to deal with that?"

"Those things are nothing more than a minor inconvenience." Monroe dismissed them with a wave of his hand. "There is nothing to directly tie me to any of those things. Rufus Manteau will be taken care of one way or another. He is not of concern to me. His handler at the FBI is no longer a threat. I don't know who killed him. It was most unfortunate. I may suffer some minor embarrassment about the hooker if any of this ever comes out and I have to deny involvement, but it's nothing I can't withstand, just a minor speed bump in the road."

"Okay," Ben said. "I'll take you at your word. Let this be a test. We will soon find out if loyalty is something that should be shared between us."

The door opened, and two waiters bustled in and set antipasto salads and wine in front of them. When they were alone, Ben stood and raised his glass of Chianti. "Salute," he said, and he exited without another word, leaving the untouched salad behind on the table.

CHAPTER 28

Dimase sat patiently with the headphones still perched atop his head. Ben would exit the restaurant shortly and walk the two blocks to Dimase's van. Dimase had operatives in the street as well as in three different cars. They were set up to trail Monroe by switching off at different points in order to avoid being recognized. Dimase's people had arrived early and blanketed the area around Fiola. When Monroe had entered the restaurant, his driver had parked around the corner and walked to a nearby Starbucks.

Dimase had been hoping for just such an opportunity. One of his men had pretended to cross the street and, when he was just behind Monroe's limousine, dropped a briefcase full of papers. As he'd bent over to scoop them up, he'd quickly reached under the bumper and attached a magnetic tracking device to the chassis of the vehicle.

"Bug attached," Dimase had heard through his headphones as he monitored communication in the back of the van. He'd smiled to himself. So much for Monroe making evasive turns and abrupt changes of direction. With three tracking vehicles, they should be able to keep up with him now.

As Ben approached the van, one of Dimase's operatives on the sidewalk scratched his nose in a prearranged signal to indicate that Ben had not been followed upon leaving the restaurant. Immediately,

Ben pulled open the passenger-side door and jumped into the van. The driver, wearing an earpiece, acknowledged him with quick thumbs-up.

Dimase was in back, where all the seats had been removed and replaced with an array of communication and computer equipment mounted on bolted-down steel shelving. There were two low-level swivel stools in front of a low half table, with wall shelving extending from behind and up to the van roof.

Dimase sat at one of the stools with his headphones in place and motioned for Ben to take the other stool. He momentarily slid the headphones down to his neck and gave Ben a high five. "You were unbelievable, my friend," he said. "You played him like a fiddle."

"Thanks," Ben replied. "Did you get it all?"

"Every bit. The guy is a psycho, but he's obviously very dangerous. Several people have already lost their lives, and who knows how many others might have died in the past that we don't know about? He'll clearly stop at nothing to get what he wants."

"I agree," Ben said. "He really thinks he's going to be a god on earth, to use his words. He thinks he's going to rule the world, first from the shadows and then out in the open. I wonder how large his group actually is."

"I don't know," Dimase replied, "but seeing how he reacted to your proposal of being a consultant on your Manhattan project, he's probably been laundering all kinds of money in many different ways and for many years. Money talks; they look for people who are discontented, feel passed over, or believe that the country is irreversibly headed in the wrong direction and that they are owed something. In some cases, people who already have a criminal disposition from the start are easily corrupted if the right situation presents itself."

Ben shook his head. "I imagine some in his network are true believers convinced they can pull off a relatively bloodless coup. Others may be in so far over their heads after accepting money or performing illegal acts that they can't turn back."

Dimase patted his friend on the shoulder. "Whatever the individual motivation, it's clear he has some level of organization, and we have to assume they've penetrated the FBI, possibly other government agencies and law enforcement, certain elected officials and bureaucrats, and some people in the business community. You turned the tables on him when you tried to recruit him. That was brilliant."

"Yeah, well, it was just a spur-of-the-moment reaction, but it got him to reveal something, so that's good. Do you think that would be enough to get a conviction?"

"Not by itself," Dimase replied. "Obviously, his saying it's on a need-to-know basis implies that he knows and you don't need to know. The same with his statement that he would not tell you who the target is 'for your own protection.' Those are pretty incriminating statements—good for purposes of our investigation but probably not admissible in court. We don't have a warrant. We recorded him without his knowledge. Really, the only advantage of these tapes is whatever information we get to help take him down. Hopefully, if we can nail him, there will be enough other evidence throughout that process that these tapes will never become an issue."

"So where do we go from here?" Ben asked. "We know there is a target, and we know the timetable is next week. What do you think?"

"I think that tells us a lot," Dimase replied. "I was thinking Operation SCOTUS might have something to do with the death of Justice Thompkins a few weeks ago. Even though everyone seemed to agree at the time that he died of natural causes, I wonder if somehow he could have been murdered, and Cady found out about it. That theory would pretty much explain everything that happened. Monroe ordered a hit on her to tie up that loose end. For some reason, this Rufus Manteau character attacked your Acadia first. The only reason we've come up with so far for that is to make it look like a local mystery, with people of the same name getting bumped off, and to divert attention away from the angle that the hooker was a Washington-ordered hit. Then Manteau went to the hospital to finish off Acadia, but he got interrupted and killed three people in the process. Manteau is on the run. Someone in the FBI was afraid that if he got caught, he would identify his local handler at the FBI, so the FBI murdered their own guy to sever the connection. That means Manteau is no longer a threat to them. It also means we're looking for one or more people higher up in the FBI who ordered and executed a hit on their own guy."

Ben shook his head and let out a long breath. "That would explain everything except for the fact that there is still a target out there, and the timetable for that target is next week, so Operation SCOTUS has to have more involved than just the death of Thompkins, whatever the cause."

"So Operation SCOTUS either has more than one piece, or it has yet to occur at all."

"Who do you think the target could be?" Ben asked.

"It has to be a Supreme Court justice, right?" Dimase said. "That's why they called it Operation SCOTUS. If it wasn't Thompkins, then it has to be one of the eight justices left. That conclusion still fits all the facts; it's just an extension of our working theory of what's happened, an additional piece of the operation."

"I agree," Ben said. "I think we have to assume that Monroe is behind a plot to assassinate another justice and that it is set to take place next week." He swiveled on his stool. "But who?"

CHAPTER
29

Monroe remained seated at the table in the private room at Fiola. His meeting with Ben had indeed led to an unexpected development. Ben Johnson did not appear to be as squeaky clean as he'd first thought. He was going to be either a formidable adversary or a valuable ally. He certainly knew enough to be dangerous to Monroe and his associates if that was his intention.

Extreme caution would have to be exercised from that point forward. Johnson must have had extensive connections to know all the things he'd brought up. Most troubling was the hit on the FBI handler in Alexandria. He seemed to suspect that persons higher up in the FBI had ordered the hit to protect themselves and others in the chain of command. Johnson knew all about Rufus Manteau and had implied that Monroe himself had ordered the hit on the hooker, triggering the entire sequence of events.

How could Johnson have known all of that? Monroe was baffled—and worried. As far as Monroe knew, the only reason the authorities might look at him for anything was whatever Cady LaFleur might have written in her diary, and she certainly hadn't known any details about Operation SCOTUS. She probably hadn't even known what SCOTUS was.

Francois had already warned Monroe that the authorities would be looking at him for the hooker hit, but he hadn't mentioned anything about SCOTUS. It was Francois who'd speculated that SCOTUS was now operational, and Francois had been at the retreat where they'd conceived the then hypothetical idea. The detective who'd approached Francois apparently hadn't mentioned anything about SCOTUS. How would he have known? He couldn't have. Francois had recognized the scenario when Thompkins died. He had been the one who asked if SCOTUS was in play.

So where had Johnson gotten such specific information? Was it possible he had some sort of contact within Monroe's operational circle of SCOTUS? Could it have been Harrington? Monroe himself did not know the names of the agents who would take Sumner out. That was Harrington's purview. What were the odds that Harrington was Johnson's contact? Harrington had been around for a long time. Could he have been working both sides of the fence in some fashion?

Monroe sent Harrington a text, exited Fiola, and climbed into the back of his limo. He gave the driver instructions and settled back to think, too worried to even bother to look in the mirrors that time.

◆　◆　◆

As Monroe's limo pulled away from the curb, one of Dimase's men maneuvered his own vehicle into the line of traffic, falling in place several cars back.

After two miles, the trail car broke off, taking a hard right turn, and a second vehicle coming from a side street picked up the tail. A half mile behind, Dimase and Ben Johnson followed in the van, monitoring the tracking device on a green-shaded screen.

"He's headed out on 95 North," the trail vehicle operative said through Dimase's headphones.

"Roger that," Dimase said. "Unit three, pick him up at the cutoff entrance. Unit two, break off at that point."

"Affirmative," both drivers replied in quick succession.

The new trail vehicle followed the limo for about twenty miles before the target exited at a major rest-area complex. The limo parked in a far corner of the parking lot, away from the restaurants and foot traffic, and Monroe exited and climbed into the front passenger seat of an adjacent car, a black Cadillac Escalade SUV.

"He's parked in a remote corner and entered a nearby vehicle," Dimase's man said over the radio. "It looks like the other car was waiting for him. There's no one else in the vicinity. Looks like it might be a government-registered SUV. I can't see inside the vehicle."

"Roger that," Dimase said. "Don't let them make you. If you can't get a visual on the driver, try to get a plate number."

"Will do."

Minutes later, the operative came back on the radio. "He's returned to the limo. I couldn't get any visibility, but it looks like only one guy in the Escalade. Plate US 3243."

"Roger," Dimase replied. He paused to consider what to do. They couldn't tail both vehicles, which would spread them too thin and potentially lead them to be discovered. "Unit one, are you there now?"

"Affirmative."

"Good. When the limo exits, you follow. We'll try to locate the other guy later if we can ID him through his plate number. Radio unit three when you see what direction Monroe is headed. Three, you get out ahead of them, and position yourself for a handoff. Two, you trail way back, out of visual range. After three takes the handoff, you get out ahead and position yourself for another handoff if needed. We'll be headed in your general direction with the tracker just in case he shakes loose. Meanwhile, we'll run this other plate and see what we can get."

Dimase texted the plate number to Larson with a request to run it down. Thirty minutes later, Larson reported back that it was an FBI vehicle. He couldn't tell whom it was assigned to, but he said he would reach out to a contact from his days at the FBI to see if he could call in a favor. With a lull in the action, Dimase googled "Supreme Court justices" and selected a link that provided some information.

"So which one do you think it is?" he asked Ben, printing out a list and handing it to him.

Ben scrutinized the names and said, "Unless Monroe is cooking up something really outside the box, it would have to be a conservative, right? Monroe is a longtime Democrat. Now that the party has merged with the socialists, he's been jockeying for position within the new order. Based on my conversations with him, he wants to ride the newly formed party as long and as far as he can. I don't think he gives a rat's ass about the ideology. He just sees it as an opportunity. That said, his public persona is leaning hard left. He wants to control the government, particularly the treasury. What could possibly stand in his way?"

"A conservative court," Dimase answered.

"Bingo," Ben said. "He's convinced the Democratic Socialists will control Congress and the executive branch, but they will never have complete control if a conservative Supreme Court stands in their way."

"I think you may be onto something," Dimase said. "What is the orientation of these eight?"

Ben was enough of a national player to be familiar with the political leanings of each justice and whether each had been appointed by a Republican or a Democrat. He penciled in an *R* or a *D* next to each name. "The court still leans conservative right now. It was six–three conservative until Thompkins died. He was a staunch conservative. Now it's still five–three conservative, with an appointment pending. Obviously, the current president will appoint a liberal, but that would still leave a five–four conservative majority."

"That must be it!" Dimase exclaimed. "Think about it. If Operation SCOTUS is meant to take out one of the conservative justices, it would swing the balance the other way. If the current president can appoint two liberals, the court will have gone from a six–three conservative majority to a five–four liberal majority."

"I think you're right," Ben said, "but if this was all by design, how did they kill Thompkins and get away with it?"

"Maybe they didn't kill Thompkins. After all, both sides signed off on the autopsy and investigation. There was no question at the time that he died of natural causes." Dimase lit a cigarette. "But what if the entire operation was contingent upon Thompkins dying? He was eighty-six and in poor health. He had to go sooner or later. What if Monroe and his people had Operation SCOTUS all set up in advance, and Thompkins's natural death was the triggering event? They couldn't just recklessly start murdering Supreme Court justices, but if one went on his own, could they get away with murdering one justice?"

"There'd still be a hell of a stink," Ben said. "It would take brass balls to pull it off."

"Perhaps, but it depends on how they do it. Also, they would exert heavy influence over any investigation, possibly even outright control. We already know the FBI has been compromised at some level. The Democratic Socialists already control the House and the presidency. It would not be in their best interest to push too hard on any inquiry. Of course, they would have to make it look good, but could they look the other way on certain things?"

"That's got to be it," Ben said. "It would fit with everything else. Monroe even said to me that when they controlled the entire government, they would step out of the shadows."

"So if our theory is correct, who would it be? Who is the target?"

Ben thought for a moment and crossed out the three names on the list with a *D* next to them. "We can exclude these right off the bat."

"What are the ages of the five remaining conservatives?" Dimase asked.

Ben again looked over the list and penciled in some numbers. "This guy has been around forever," he said, indicating with his pencil. "He's seventy-five. The three conservatives appointed from the last presidential term are fifty-eight, fifty-four, and forty-five. Sumner is by far the youngest. He's only midforties."

"So if you were Monroe and you wanted as much insurance as possible that any change to the court's balance would be long term, would you not go after the youngest conservative? Would you not make Sumner your target?"

"It has to be him."

Just then, Dimase's phone pinged with a new text from Bill Larson: "My contact at FBI checked computer records for me. I owe her one. Plate is for car assigned to Frank Harrington, assistant deputy director."

Dimase held the phone so Ben could read the text. "I believe we have just identified Monroe's primary contact at the FBI."

CHAPTER
30

Frank Harrington was losing his nerve. He always had seen himself as a hard-ass, and he hated that he was so anxious and hated the corrupt person he had become. To make matters worse, he no longer trusted Monroe. The man knew no such thing as loyalty. He was too quick to write off his own people as collateral damage. Harrington had to wonder if he too would soon become collateral damage.

Monroe clearly had not been himself at the last rest-stop meeting. The mounting pressure and recent screwups were ratcheting up the stress level on all of them, but Monroe had just let loose on him like a wild animal backed into a corner. He practically had accused Harrington of working for someone else and of deliberately orchestrating the mess in Alexandria to sabotage Monroe and point the authorities in his direction. The man was losing touch with reality.

As Harrington drove, he noticed his left triceps began to twitch, and the fingers on his left hand started to tremble. He shook his arm and flexed his fingers, but the involuntary movements persisted. He gripped the steering wheel like a vise and steered his car to the middle lane of the highway. Beads of sweat appeared above his upper lip, and his vision seemed to go in and out of focus.

He punched a button on the Escalade's dashboard to max out the fan and air-conditioning and shook his head in an attempt to clear his vision and regain focus. Nothing helped. He felt as if he couldn't breathe. A heavy weight started to press against his chest. Was he having a heart attack? His breathing grew shallow and rapid. The shaking would not stop.

Cars started to streak past him on both sides; some blasted horns as they blew by. His brain was a jumble of thoughts, mostly trying to concentrate on the immediacy of breathing and trying to maneuver the Cadillac over to the emergency lane. He struggled to check the side and rearview mirrors for an opening to slide right, not realizing his speed had dropped to twenty miles per hour. Finally, he yanked the wheel hard, turned sharply into the emergency lane, and rolled to a stop as far off the highway as possible. Harrington slumped in his seat, wondering if that was where he would die.

Within a few minutes, his breathing grew deeper, and the pressure in his chest began to subside. He gulped down most of a bottle of water kept in the cup holder. He held out his left arm and extended his fingers to check for shaking, but the tremors had stopped. He still had the engine running with the air-conditioning on full blast. He took a napkin from the glove compartment, soaked it with the remaining water in the bottom of the bottle, and patted down his face, taking long, deep, controlled breaths as he did so.

What was that? At first, he'd thought it was a heart attack, but now he didn't think so. He was pretty much back to normal. The stress was getting to him. In many ways, he was between a rock and a hard place, with limited options. He had never experienced anything like the episode that had just occurred. It was difficult to admit, but he was pretty sure he'd just had an anxiety attack.

Harrington angled the vent toward him. Operation SCOTUS was still on, but then what? Harrington was no longer confident in Monroe or in the long-term outcome Monroe envisioned.

When Monroe first had recruited him five years ago, the timing had been perfect. Monroe was on the congressional committee responsible for FBI and Justice Department oversight. Harrington was career FBI and, in all likelihood, had risen about as high as he would ever go as assistant deputy director. There were two people in the upper echelon at the bureau who were clear favorites for promotion to the top, and he was not one of them.

Eventually, the senator had disclosed bits and pieces of his grand vision and shared that there were others in high places who were with him. Harrington had witnessed the politicization of the FBI and Justice Department over the years, and it sickened him. Monroe's ideas made sense, and the more they'd discussed them, the more appealing the senator's worldview had become.

The initial small favors had been followed by larger tasks, often accompanied by generous bonus payments made to offshore accounts in the Cayman Islands or Switzerland. Most of Harrington's assignments had centered on recruitment of other FBI and law enforcement personnel. There had been an occasional request for confidential information and, once or twice, a little informal intimidation of political or business types at Monroe's behest but no murder or assassinations. Recruitment, provision of low-level muscle, and occasional extortion had been the roles Harrington fulfilled as he built his own network within Monroe's larger, loosely formed organization.

Then along had come Operation SCOTUS. By the time Monroe and some of his political buddies had cooked up SCOTUS, Harrington's offshore accounts had stood at just about $1.5 million. He was in deep, and there was no turning back. The only path for him was to see Monroe's vision through to fruition. If it came true, Harrington would have more than he'd ever dreamed of. If it didn't, he knew he would get destroyed along the way.

But the FBI agent hit was the first time Harrington had been asked to actually kill people. Now four people had died, with more likely to come. He had been forced to kill one of his own, someone he'd recruited. That did not sit well with him, but that was the least of his worries at the moment.

Monroe was his main concern. The man was running scared. Ben Johnson's knowledge of Operation SCOTUS and all the craziness in Alexandria had Monroe spooked. He was questioning Harrington's loyalty. Based on Monroe's track record, that did not bode well for Harrington's longevity.

Harrington wondered if Monroe had other operatives out there he didn't know about, operatives like himself—capable of murder. Many open investigations were moving in Monroe's direction. Wouldn't it make sense for him to eliminate Harrington and pin it all on him?

Yes, a rock and a hard place for sure. Monroe would always be a threat to him, whether or not Operation SCOTUS was successful. Harrington could no longer trust him. Once Monroe got what he wanted, Harrington would be expendable, and it would be expeditious from Monroe's point of view to get rid of him.

Harrington wondered how extensive Monroe's network was. If one cut off the head, would the organization simply disappear, or would a new leader emerge to continue the agenda?

A plan began to form in Harrington's head. There was a way forward for him. It was a narrow opening but possible.

Harrington resolved to make a run for it. The key would be the timing. He also resolved to take a page out of Monroe's book: Monroe had to go.

CHAPTER 31

After the anxiety attack passed, Harrington drove west, picking up Route 66 toward Virginia. Eventually, he exited onto 234 North toward Catharpin, Virginia, working his way into farm country. After about fifteen miles, he navigated some secondary roads and came to the long, hard-packed dirt drive he was looking for.

Harrington had rented the old farmhouse and barn about six months earlier in anticipation of needing an operations center if Operation SCOTUS ever went live. The property suited his needs perfectly; the house was set back hundreds of feet from the road, with the barn located behind.

He drove down the long driveway, past rolling fields and faded post fencing. The property had been a working farm for generations before falling into disrepair after the family patriarch died of old age and none of his descendants had a desire to continue the family tradition. His three children and their children had long since moved to the suburbs and were scattered all up and down the East Coast. They were only too happy to rent out the property while they contemplated how to carve it up and maximize the value.

Harrington pulled around the house and parked in front of the barn, out of sight from the road. Andrews and Spivka were waiting for him inside the barn, putting the final touches on a fake UPS truck.

"It looks good," Harrington said as he entered the barn through a side door. He had authorized the two agents to requisition UPS stencils and uniforms from the undercover operations center at Quantico. No one had given the order a second thought, as the requisition had had the signature of the assistant deputy director.

"Yeah," Spivka replied. "I suppose if you put it side by side with a real one, you might notice the difference, but for our purposes, it will do nicely."

Harrington nodded, admiring their work. Spivka had taken two personal days to drive to Georgia, make a cash purchase of the used box truck at a small-time secondhand lot, and drive it anonymously back to the barn in Virginia. His partner, Andrews, had stolen a pair of commercial plates, which were now affixed to the back of the truck. Andrews also had filed away the vehicle identification number.

As an extra precaution, the two agents took care to wear gloves whenever they were working in and around the truck. When they were done with the current assignment, they'd made arrangements to deliver the truck to a salvage yard operated by a member of their network, where the truck would be immediately dismantled and destroyed. Within twenty-four hours of Operation SCOTUS being executed, the truck would cease to exist and, for all practical purposes, would never have existed.

Andrews came from around the side of the truck and shook Harrington's hand. "Any word on when we go?" he asked.

"Yes," Harrington replied. "We're green for next Tuesday. Are you both ready?"

"Ready as we'll ever be." Spivka answered for both of them. "We just want to get it over with."

"Good. Me too," Harrington said. "Let's go over it one more time."

"Right," Andrews said. The two FBI agents had been partners for so long that they often seamlessly spoke for one another. "Subject target typically goes for a jog at 0530 each morning. We will position the truck about two blocks away to the east, with a clear sight line to the target's front door. Ideally, we'll be far enough away that the target will not notice us. If he does see the truck, most likely, he'll assume we are in a holding position, waiting until we can make an early morning delivery somewhere. Either way, we'll be several hundred feet away, and he'll be taking off in the opposite direction."

Spivka took up the narrative. "Target is typically gone for twenty-five minutes. While he's gone, we'll move the truck up to be parked in front of the house immediately east and adjacent to the target's home. As the target returns to his own driveway and approaches his front door, I will exit the truck and time my approach to be within twenty feet right after he opens the door. I will wave a delivery slip in my hand and ask if he knows where the address is."

Andrews jumped back in. "As the target's attention is drawn toward Spivka, I will exit the truck and move rapidly toward the target's front door. Spivka will get there first and engage the target in conversation, attempting to get him to look at the delivery slip. Spivka's priority is to not let the door close and lock, even if he has to put his foot in the door for a second or two until I get there. Once I arrive, we will force the target into the house and close the door. We will exercise extreme caution not to strike or bruise the target. I will attempt to bear-hug the target, pinning his arms to his sides, while Spivka administers a sleep hold. Once the target is unconscious, we will prop open his mouth with a small block, gently pull his tongue out with pliers, and administer the fatal dose of succinylcholine on the underside of the base of the tongue."

Spivka continued the recital. "We'll take care to make sure the position of the body and the overall scene are consistent with the target collapsing from a heart attack after just reentering the house. We will casually exit the house and drive directly to the salvage yard, where we will dispose of the truck, and you will pick us up."

"Good," Harrington said. "What do you do if a witness is present?"

"We must make a decision as to whether we should abort and evacuate or continue the mission." Spivka replied. "The mission will be compromised if it can be determined that the target was assassinated and did not die of natural causes. If we have a nonconfrontational witness outside the house, we act casual—business as usual—and leave, as long as the witness gives no indication he or she is aware of anything being wrong. If a witness questions us directly or takes specific notice, we will take the witness with us and arrange for anonymous disposal in order to not jeopardize the operation."

"Okay." Harrington smiled. "I've got something for you." He opened a briefcase he'd brought in from the Escalade and removed an iPad. He went through a series of keystrokes and showed the men an electronic confirmation that $400,000 had been deposited for each of them in a series of offshore accounts. He also removed two packets of bundled cash from the briefcase. "As agreed, here is twenty-five thousand dollars for each of you in unmarked hundreds. This will hold you over for the time being; don't spend it all in one place. After the mission is successfully completed, there will be another three hundred seventy-five thousand deposited for each of you in your offshore accounts." Harrington had no intention of ever depositing that money, but that was not something Spivka and Andrews had to know. If things went according to plan, he would be long gone by then.

◆　◆　◆

Boston, Massachusetts

Four hundred seventy-three miles away, in the Boston offices of Augustin and Larson Confidential LLC, Bill Larson was searching through commercial flight manifests for flights between Washington, DC, and Louisiana during the forty-eight-hour period prior to the murder of the FBI agent in Alexandria. His contact at the FBI had accessed the airline logs and faxed them over to him. He didn't want to mention Harrington's name to her, thinking it would be better to do the search himself. After all, the name he was looking for was the assistant deputy director and was her boss. There was no need to put her in any jeopardy.

Earlier, she had checked records to see if the FBI had authorized any private flights, but no FBI personnel had flown in government aircraft on those dates between those locations, so there was no list of names from that source to review. At first, Larson didn't find what he was looking for on the commercial manifests either. He came up empty for flights between DC-area airports and Alexandria. Then he expanded his search radius in Louisiana to include New Orleans.

"Well, well, well. What have we here?" Larson said.

There it was: Frank Harrington had flown from DC to New Orleans and back again in one day—the same day the FBI agent in Alexandria had been murdered. Larson did the math in his head and confirmed that Harrington had had plenty of time to land in New Orleans, rent a car, drive to Alexandria and back, and catch a late-afternoon flight back to DC.

There was no doubt in his mind that Harrington was dirty. He must have felt some significant exposure to be desperate enough to take out his own agent and to do the job himself. If true, that would prove Harrington was more than just an FBI contact for Monroe. He was operational.

Larson pumped his fist in triumph. He had to get in touch with Dimase. Harrington was the key. Circumstantial evidence made Harrington the odds-on favorite to be the tactical head of Operation SCOTUS.

CHAPTER 32

Dimase and Ben were huddled around the conference table in Ben's suite at the Hyatt Regency on Capitol Hill. Dimase had a line chart sketched out in black marker on the pad in front of him and was repeatedly circling the name Harrington. The drawing looked like an organizational chart for any typical business, with Senator Richard Monroe at the top, a line to Harrington beneath him, and an arrow pointing down from there to the heading "Operation SCOTUS."

They knew a lot, but they didn't know enough, and their hands were tied for fear of the FBI being compromised. In all likelihood, the blanks they wanted to fill in—the field operatives tasked with taking out Sumner—were FBI agents or contractors themselves.

"We're going to go on the assumption that Sumner is the target, and we know the hit is next week. We don't know where, how, or specifically when," Dimase said.

"How high do you think this goes? Do you think the president is in on it?" Ben asked.

"There is no way to tell; whether knowingly or not, he's a key participant because he would name the next two justices, both for Thompkins and for Sumner. God help us if he does know about it. That would be a coup d'état with one branch of the government taking over another. If that is the case, we have to assume the corruption could extend far beyond the FBI. Right now, we can't trust any level of law enforcement. We have to go it alone and then try to expose the plot to the light of day. It's our best shot."

"We can't cover Sumner twenty-four-seven ourselves," Ben replied. "Even with all your resources, once the Secret Service picks him up for work in the morning, he's pretty much beyond our reach."

"True," Dimase said. "In order to have a chance, we have to make some assumptions. I don't think a public assassination is likely. That could implicate the Secret Service, and the last thing that would serve their purposes would be to have a political assassination. They must make it appear to be at least plausible that Sumner's death is unrelated to politics—some sort of accident or random violence. They can't just have a Secret Service agent turn around and shoot him in the car on the way home from work. He's probably pretty safe when he's at the Supreme Court. That means they would have to strike when he's on his own time, most likely at home or perhaps if he has some kind of trip or vacation planned."

Ben thought about that. "It's easy enough to check the itinerary for the court for next week. If they are in session, he won't be going anywhere. I suppose he could have an evening function of some sort."

"Yes, but Secret Service would accompany him to any local functions."

"True, so by process of elimination, the attack would take place at his house, either in the evening or in early morning. Why don't we just approach him and warn him and set up some kind of defense?"

"He doesn't know us," Dimase said. "We can't just walk up and ring his doorbell. I'm sure if we were able to speak with him at all, he would immediately notify and engage the Secret Service, and they in turn would bring the FBI into the loop. If any of those agents are compromised, we would have tipped our hand, and they'd change the plan. I don't see how we can credibly approach him directly, and I don't see how we can go through official channels without risking everything."

"You have enough manpower to stake out his house, right?" Ben asked. "We could at least do that."

"Yes, we could do that, but could we be close enough to intervene and still not be seen? It is very difficult to do if we don't know who is coming and when and how."

Ben thought for a moment. "I have an idea. What if I can get Monroe to tell us?"

"How would you propose to do that?" Dimase asked.

"What time is it?"

"Two o'clock."

"We've got eyes on Monroe, right? What if we send one of your guys right up to him and hand him a note? Pretend the messenger is part of my network and push the envelope even further with the notion that I have sources everywhere and know a lot more than he thinks?"

"What would the note say?"

"How about something short and shocking, designed to get him to drop everything and meet with me right away? He doesn't know that we've identified Harrington as his FBI contact and probable tactical head of Operation SCOTUS. Your guy could hand him an urgent note from me."

"They have security, Ben. How would we get the note past security?"

"Well, we'll mark it as personal. And when he sees my name, he'll open it right away. The note can be along the lines that Harrington has been turned and is an extreme threat to him. I'll say that we must meet immediately—tonight. I'll get him talking. He'll be scared shit, and it will drive him crazy that I know about Harrington after I already blew his mind at lunch by bringing up Operation SCOTUS. You can wire me. We'll pick the rendezvous place. I'll lay it on the line with him that it's either Harrington's ass or his. He won't understand how I could possibly know about Harrington. He'll assume the entire operation is in jeopardy. I'll offer him a solution, but for my people to execute that solution, he has to take me into his confidence. Dimase, I think he is ripe. I had him on his heels earlier. I think I can pull this off."

Dimase did not appear to be as confident. "It is a lot of risk for you, my friend. There are many things that could go wrong. You are not a cop."

"I want this guy bad," Ben replied. "I'm a big boy, Dimase. I've been around the block a couple times. I know what I'm doing. Maybe I'm tougher than you think."

"I do not question your toughness, Ben, but what if he just picks up the phone the moment you leave and orders a hit on you?"

"We'll take precautions. Look, I won't be alone. I need to do this for Acadia. Dimase, I'm not asking for your permission; I'm only asking for your help."

◆　◆　◆

Ninety minutes later, one of Dimase's men entered the Russell Senate Office Building and made his way to Senator Monroe's second-floor office. He approached the receptionist with a sealed envelope in his hand. The envelope was marked, "Urgent—personal and confidential," and it was addressed to Senator Monroe from Ben Johnson.

"Excuse me," Dimase's man said as the receptionist looked up. "I have an urgent personal message for Senator Monroe. It is imperative that he read this message immediately."

"That's highly irregular," the receptionist replied. "All envelopes have to be screened by security first."

"He will want to read this. It's a matter of national security and of the highest priority. If you tell him the message is from Ben Johnson, he will understand."

"I don't know," the receptionist said hesitantly. "I have specific orders he's not to be disturbed. He's on a very important conference call."

"Ma'am, all due respect, why don't you let him make the decision? When he does get the message, if he finds that you delayed his getting it, he will be very angry with you. Trust me—take thirty seconds, and give him the option."

The woman looked troubled but took the envelope and went through a door to the inner office. Two minutes later, she returned, looking relieved. "He said to tell you that he understands and will take care of it."

"Thank you," the man said, and he left. Once out on the sidewalk, he called Dimase on his cell. "Message delivered. He said he understands and will take care of it."

"Excellent. Good work," Dimase replied. Smiling at Ben Johnson, he said, "I think he took the bait. Let's get ready to roll."

CHAPTER 33

For the second time in six hours, Ben Johnson and Senator Monroe sat across from one another. There had been a subtle shift in the power dynamic. This time, instead of meeting on neutral turf, Monroe had come willingly to Ben's suite on the penthouse level of the Hyatt Regency on Capitol Hill.

Monroe appeared to be mildly agitated and anxious as Ben poured him a drink and placed it on the coffee table in front of him. Ben was in no hurry to speak, electing to allow the tension to build after initially greeting the senator and offering him a seat. Monroe's body language did not exude the same level of confidence he'd shown earlier in the day at Fiola, when his goal had been to recruit Ben.

The senator looked uncomfortable and ill at ease. Ben secretly hoped he had been feeling that way all afternoon since Ben had turned the tables on him at their earlier luncheon meeting and then abruptly left. Ben figured Monroe must have been wondering just how extensive Ben's network of sources, contacts, and contractors really was. Hopefully the note that had lured him there had him questioning the loyalty of his own people, particularly Harrington. Ben hoped he could exploit Monroe's uncertainty and that the two of them could find common ground. The senator already knew that Ben was well known and well connected in both business and political circles. Now

Ben had to convince him that he also had an intelligence operation and clandestine organization at his disposal, working surreptitiously behind the scenes on his behalf.

At lunch, Monroe had suggested they join forces. By the time he left that meeting, Ben wanted Monroe to be fearful about who would have the controlling hand in such an alliance. Monroe finally broke the silence as it became obvious Ben was measuring him, waiting for him to speak.

"How do you know about Harrington?" Monroe asked.

"I told you at lunch, Senator. I have my own network—older, larger, and obviously more effective than yours." Ben paused to let that comment sink in. "You offered me a partnership at lunch. You describe a grand vision wherein you control the government, and my firm is one of your conduits for siphoning the treasury and laundering billions of dollars. Did you really think I would be subordinate in such a relationship, Dickie?"

The senator involuntarily flinched at the use of his nickname.

Ben continued. "I've been around this town a lot longer than you, Senator. I've made a lot more money and a lot more friends. You and your people could be a nice complementary piece for me."

"You would still need me politically, no matter what other connections you have," Monroe said. "You're not in position to be elected or to run the government. You're in the private sector."

"It is I who own the politicians," Ben said, "not the other way around. I've been trying to demonstrate that to you. Do you still believe you should trust that stooge Harrington more than you trust me? At lunch, you spoke of having a few gold coins in your pocket and offering me one. Let me assure you, Senator, it is I who am offering you the gold coin, and I sincerely hope you take it. I am offering you a chance for survival—a chance for your grand scheme to become reality. If I sat back and remained silent, you would not be alive in a few days' time. It is I who am extending my hand to you in exchange for your loyalty."

Monroe sat mute, staring at Ben and gripping his glass with both hands.

"Yes," Ben said, "if we do it right, you will work the political side, and I will stay in the shadows, but make no mistake: I will be the one calling the shots. You will be right there with me. All your dreams of power and wealth will come true. We will both be global in stature. Nothing will be beyond our reach, but you must trust me and swear your loyalty. That is the only way this will work. My terms are unconditional. Join me, and we will triumph together. Walk away, and you will perish."

"Perish?" Monroe stammered. "What do you know? What are you saying?"

"Very well, Senator. I will give you something, and when I'm finished, you will have to decide. You will either get up and leave this room and go your own way, or you will accept my terms and trust in my judgment."

"Go on," Monroe said as he took a long sip from his drink. "I'm listening."

"Consider this, Senator. I know that Frank Harrington is your main contact at the FBI. I know that among other things, he runs a network of corrupt agents on your behalf, including the agent in Alexandria whom he personally murdered in an attempt to protect you and others further upstream in your group. To protect you from any further implications in the murder of Cady LaFleur, a young hooker you know very well, who saw a text on your phone about Operation SCOTUS. Senator, I know that Justice Sumner is the target, and you've already told me the hit is scheduled for next week. I believe it will take place at his home. Is that enough, or do you want more?"

Monroe sat in stunned silence, at a loss for words.

"I also know something you don't know," Ben said. "My sources tell me Harrington has turned. He's going to see Operation SCOTUS through, probably for financial reasons and because he's in so deep that there is no turning back for him. Then he's going to come for you. Ask yourself a question, Senator. If you take Harrington and his own network of FBI agents and low-level contractors out of the picture, who do you have left to protect you? If all those guys are suddenly against you and no longer doing your bidding through Harrington, who stands between them and you? Your driver? Anyone?"

"How can you possibly know all this?" Monroe asked. He looked like a deer in headlights.

"Have I been off so far? I'm offering you a way out," Ben said. "The only way out, if you think about it."

"I'm still listening," Monroe replied.

"I believe it is in both of our interests to see Operation SCOTUS through to fruition. We should let Harrington complete his mission. When he is done, my people will erase him. The trail will end with him. The risk will be eliminated. With Harrington gone, you and I will both be clean. We will be in positon to move forward with your agenda. The court will no longer be an obstacle. Your political contacts will be in place. Eventually, we will control all aspects of the government. There will be nothing to prevent us from accomplishing what you have described to me."

Senator Monroe nodded as he considered the new angle.

Ben went on. "If you don't want to follow my suggestion, I doubt you will be alive in two weeks. It may be Harrington, or it may be one of his people, but they will come for you."

"I've had my doubts about Harrington," Monroe said softly.

"Do you know which FBI agents he has working with him? How many? Who they are?"

"No," Monroe replied. "That was all his setup. I had no need to know specific names. Anything I needed done was funneled through Harrington. I kept myself insulated from anything dirty."

"For Operation SCOTUS to succeed, and to protect you in the aftermath, we must identify Harrington's operatives."

"How can you do that?" Monroe asked.

"There is only one way," Ben replied. "I've given you more than enough to prove you can trust me. If we did not have a common goal, I would go to Sumner and to the authorities, and I would blow up the entire operation. Our interests are aligned, Senator. I want Operation SCOTUS to succeed. I want you in political power. I want to utilize your network of political contacts, to add them to mine in both the political arena and the private sector. I agree with you that the country is changing. If we want to stay on top, we must change with it. We must adapt. We will adapt. Everything we've discussed is right there for the taking, but we must take down Harrington and any of his immediate operatives after the operation is complete. My people have to babysit Operation SCOTUS."

"Babysit?" Monroe asked.

"Yes, I already know who the target is, but I need to know specifically when, where, and how. I need you to tell me what you know, Senator. My people can then shadow the operation, make sure it is successfully carried out, and identify who is working with Harrington. When the time is right—ideally within forty-eight hours—we will clean everything up and eliminate any loose ends. So what will it be, Senator? Do you want to get up and walk out, or will you tell me when, where, and how?"

◆　◆　◆

Dimase Augustin sat hidden in one of the bedroom suites, monitoring and recording the conversation. Ben's performance was incredible. He had deftly maneuvered Senator Monroe into a corner. Dimase held his breath.

◆　◆　◆

"Okay," Monroe said, forcing a smile. "You've made your case. I guess we will sink or swim together. It will be safer and cleaner for us if he is no longer a threat."

Ben repeated the question. "When, where, and how?"

Monroe sighed. Finally, he looked Ben in the eye. "Next Tuesday morning. Early. Sumner goes for a run every morning about five thirty. He's usually gone about twenty-five minutes. Next Tuesday, when he returns, two agents dressed as UPS workers will be parked nearby in a fake UPS truck. They will intercept him at his door and force their way inside. The plan is to put a sleep hold on him without marking him. Once he is unconscious, they plan to administer some sort of poison that Harrington came up with. If all goes well, it's meant to look like Sumner had a heart attack after his run."

Ben reached across the table and shook Monroe's hand. "Okay, partner, my people will monitor the operation. Afterward, we will keep eyes on Harrington and the agents. When the opportunity presents itself, we will take care of them and tie up any loose ends. Do you expect Harrington to be there?"

"I'm not sure. I don't know exactly where he will be."

"That's all right," Ben said. "If he's not there, we'll locate him later on."

◆ ◆ ◆

In the bedroom suite, Dimase pumped his fist. "Bingo," he said softly out loud. "Got him."

CHAPTER 34

Atlanta, Georgia

A lphonse LaFleur sat somberly in a chair next to Acadia's bed at the medical facility in Georgia. As requested by Dimase, he, Clement II, and Babette had stayed away for a few days. Of course, Alphonse now knew the true story of how and why his wife had been attacked, and he realized that no one would be coming for her.

The whole thing had been a major fuckup by Rufus Manteau. There had been no elaborate scheme to use Acadia as a decoy to cover up the murder of Cady LaFleur, the hooker. Despite what Dimase Augustin had told him, the simple truth was that it had been a case of mistaken identity. Rufus Manteau had attacked the wrong woman, thinking she was the Acadia LaFleur he was supposed to murder, in an unbelievable, random coincidence and stroke of bad luck.

Alphonse's anger had subsided somewhat. He was angry at the world, but he no longer felt that Dick Monroe had intentionally abused and disrespected his family. He looked at his wife in the hospital bed. Her leg was no longer elevated, and the bruising and swelling had started to heal. She was still on an IV and a breathing machine, but some of the wires and tubing had been removed, and with the sheets pulled up around her neck, she looked as if she were sleeping peacefully and might wake up at any moment.

Alphonse felt it was his husbandly duty to hold her hand and tell her everything would be all right, but he couldn't bring himself to do it. He wanted to feel pain, loss, and regret, but he felt nothing. They had been emotionally estranged for so many years that he couldn't bring himself to feel anything. In many ways, the woman sleeping before him was a stranger. He was ambivalent to her present condition, feeling neither grief nor hope.

The anger he'd felt earlier had been from perceived disrespect toward his own stature and the family name, not from any profound sense of loss. He respected his wife but didn't love her. Still, he wondered if she would ever recover or if she would stay in that vegetative state indefinitely, perhaps for years on end. The doctors had told him there was no way of knowing. It could go either way. They had seen cases in which people in Acadia's condition suddenly had stirred awake after years in a coma and acted as if they'd just woken up from a nap. They also had cautioned him that it was just as likely she might never wake up.

Alphonse had read somewhere that people in a coma could hear others talking and sometimes understand what was being said; they just couldn't respond. He'd seen movies in which loved ones read books out loud or even sang songs to their sleeping family member. He could do none of those things. Alphonse was sure Clement II and Babette could pick up the slack in that area.

In actuality, Alphonse came to see Acadia out of a sense of duty and family obligation, a central concept to Alphonse's worldview—that and to see firsthand what her condition was. He knew Babette was coming for a visit tomorrow, and Clement II planned to visit over the weekend. As Alphonse and Acadia had done for many years, he was just there to keep up appearances.

There was still the matter of Rufus Manteau. The fact that he'd mistakenly fucked up did not get him off the hook. In Alphonse's world, score was kept, and scores were settled. The trick would be to make sure everyone knew why Manteau had been killed but without anyone being able to prove it. It was a matter of family respect, the code by which Alphonse had been raised and by which he lived— the code from which he derived his own self-worth. Family loyalty demanded retribution—an eye for an eye and a tooth for a tooth. One way or another, Rufus Manteau would have his day of reckoning. That he was able to pledge to Acadia. That he said out loud, hoping she could hear him.

CHAPTER
35

Forest Hills, Washington, DC

Spivka and Andrews sat in the fake UPS truck, parked five hundred feet east of the Sumner residence, waiting for the target to make his appearance. They were both dressed in UPS uniforms. Spivka held a clipboard in his hand and packed a military Colt .45 pistol in a holster under his uniform. Andrews was also armed, although neither had any intention of using his weapon. If guns were drawn, it would mean the mission was in deep shit.

Andrews unconsciously fingered the syringe in his pocket, along with the small tapered wooden wedge he had customized back at the barn in Catharpin. Those were the weapons of choice for that day. Spivka glanced at his watch. He knew the target should be out any minute now. Hopefully Harrington was already on his way to the salvage yard where they would rendezvous and dispose of the truck. If all went well, two hours from then, they'd be back in civilian clothes, $375,000 richer, and on their way with Harrington to be dropped off at their own cars.

Andrews tapped Spivka on the shoulder and pointed as Justice Sumner emerged from the house and began stretching on the sidewalk.

He was wearing gym shorts, a hoodie, and sunglasses as he balanced on one leg and then the other. "Look, there he is. Get ready to move up as soon as he jogs out of sight."

Sumner finished his warm-up and took off, as expected, in the opposite direction. When he was out of sight, Andrews shifted the truck into gear and slowly rolled two blocks, coming to a stop in front of the house next door to Justice Sumner's. The men were quiet with nervous anticipation. Spivka checked his watch: about twenty minutes to go.

◆   ◆   ◆

Diagonally across the street, two houses away, Dimase Augustin lay out of sight in the fully reclined passenger seat of a late-model Chevy sedan he'd procured for the occasion. Hunched low in the driver's seat next to him was another of his operatives. A little farther down the street, on the opposite side, was another nondescript sedan, parked with two more of his men hidden within. Knowing which direction the fake UPS truck would be coming from, they didn't dare park where the truck might have a sight line down into their vehicles.

Dimase wished they could have been closer, but under the circumstances, it was the best they could do. Dimase spoke softly into his mouthpiece. "Unit three, are you in position?"

"Affirmative." Unit three consisted of two more operatives who'd parked on a parallel street and then made their way on foot through a neighbor's property to the back of the Sumner residence.

"Okay, hold there until you get my signal, and then haul ass to the front corners of the house ASAP and hold there."

"Roger that."

◆   ◆   ◆

Spivka tapped his fingers while Andrews jiggled his legs, working off nervous energy as the minutes passed slowly. Both men had had Special Forces backgrounds before entering the FBI. They had been on many missions in the past, mostly military and a few for the FBI as well. The worst part was always the calm before the storm. Once the action started, there was no time to be nervous, only time to execute what they had practiced and trained for so many times, to act and to react. Spivka pointed again as Sumner finally appeared several hundred feet away on the return leg of his run.

"All right, get ready to go," Andrews said.

Spivka grasped the door handle, watching Sumner intently, ready to time his leap from the truck and make the approach. Sumner did not seem to notice the UPS truck. That was good. He looked like a boxer on a training run, with his hoodie up and his head down, plodding ahead one foot after the other.

Sumner jogged into the driveway and stopped, bent at the waist, sucking in deep breaths. His back was toward the UPS truck. Spivka cracked the passenger door, poised to step down. Sumner's driveway was short and wide, with his house set back about a hundred feet from the street. A low stone wall ran down the right side, with an opening for steps to a landing and sidewalk leading another few feet to a small porch.

Sumner straightened up and walked down the driveway toward the sidewalk steps. Spivka opened the door and dropped noiselessly to the street. When Sumner hit the first landing, Spivka quickened his pace. Sumner lingered on the porch for a moment, fishing in the pocket of his gym shorts for a key. Spivka lurked at the bottom of the stairs, still on the driveway, perhaps twenty feet away. He had to wait until Sumner unlocked the door. The timing had to be perfect.

Spivka watched as Sumner found his key and inserted it in the lock. When the door handle started to turn, Spivka took two great steps up the sidewalk toward the landing, waving the clipboard in his hand, and called out, "Excuse me. Can you help me out? I can't find this address. I think I'm lost."

Sumner half turned as Spivka steadily closed the distance between them, continuing to ask for help. Andrews had now left the UPS truck and was taking long, rapid strides down the driveway. Spivka was coming up the three steps to the porch, still talking and directing Sumner's attention to the clipboard. Andrews came through the stone wall entrance to the sidewalk steps as he quickly approached the house, breaking into a jog.

◆　◆　◆

Across the street, Dimase held a small mirror with an angled handle, struggling to see what was happening, tilting it slightly back and forth. He wished he'd already moved his men to the corners of Sumner's residence. When Spivka made it to the porch, Dimase shifted the mirror to get a view of the truck and saw Andrews accelerating toward the house. "Go, go, go!" Dimase screamed into his mouthpiece as he burst from the car and raced toward the house.

◆　◆　◆

As Andrews raced up the steps to the landing, his partner, Spivka, was already at the front door. Justice Sumner fully turned, and Andrews saw his face beneath the hoodie for the first time. It wasn't Sumner at all! Andrews cursed out loud just as the imposter delivered a short staccato blow to the throat of Spivka, sending the rogue FBI agent to his knees. Andrews was almost to the front door, taking the steps two at a time, when he saw Spivka go down. He had no time to think, just to act and react. There was nothing to do but continue his charge. Andrews was a beast of a man. He dodged a blow on the way in and tackled the hooded imposter, crashing him into the doorframe.

◆　◆　◆

Dimase and three of his men rushed up the porch steps. Dimase launched himself at Andrews, but the man was too big to take down. Behind them, he saw Spivka had recovered enough from the initial blow to roll off the steps just as Dimase's men tried to pounce on him. As Spivka rolled, he pulled the automatic pistol from the holster against his ribs and fired off three quick shots aimed center torso at his attackers. All three went down.

Dimase continued to wrestle with the larger, stronger Andrews. The fake Sumner lay unconscious at their feet; the back of his head had struck the doorframe when Andrews tackled him. Dimase's men in position at each front corner of the house had weapons drawn but held their fire for fear of hitting their own people. Spivka took cover between the side of the porch steps and a row of hedges lining the front of the house.

By the front door, Dimase desperately tried an ankle roll, allowing gravity to drop him like a stone as he cupped his hand behind Andrews's ankle and rolled his shoulder into the front of the ankle. Andrews toppled like a falling tree. Even as he fell, Dimase scurried on top of him and delivered an open-palmed blow to the bottom of Andrew's chin. The big man was stunned but spun away to his side, grasping the syringe within his pocket. Dimase couldn't get a clear blow at his throat or nose, so he pounded short repetitive blows into the man's ear, using the base of his hand as a blunt instrument.

◆　◆　◆

Andrews pulled the syringe from his pocket and popped the cap off with his thumb. He swung his arm in a desperate, blind arc and caught Dimase in the throat. Andrews pushed down on the plunger, and the needle broke off in Dimase's neck as he reacted and pulled away.

Spivka sprayed bullets toward both corners of the house, and Dimase's men retreated, while Andrews hauled Dimase to his feet. He controlled the smaller man with an iron grip around his neck. With his free hand, Andrews drew his own automatic pistol. Spivka, seeing that Andrews had gained the upper hand, emerged from the bushes and joined his partner at the bottom of the porch steps. The two men formed up back to back with their weapons pointed at each corner of the house as Andrews dragged Dimase with them, clutching him close.

Dimase's three operatives, along with the Sumner decoy, all lay prostrate on the front porch where they had fallen. The two operatives at the corners of the house observed helplessly from a position of cover, with their options limited, as the tight formation of Andrews, Spivka, and Dimase awkwardly sailor-walked down the driveway to the UPS truck.

When they reached the truck, they worked their way around to the far side, shielded from the view of Dimase's men, and entered the truck from the driver's-side door. Spivka climbed across to the passenger seat, and Andrews shoved Dimase over to him. Dimase appeared to be conscious but unresponsive as Spivka held him close, using him as a human shield.

Andrews put the idling engine in gear and raced off as fast as the truck would go. "What the hell was that?" he shouted once they'd cleared the immediate area. In the distance, they could hear police sirens growing louder, probably spurred by reports of gunfire.

"It was a setup!" Spivka yelled back. "They were waiting for us."

"No shit," Andrews replied. "You think Harrington knew?"

"I don't know. I don't think so. Why would he do that?"

"What do we do now?" Andrews asked.

"We've got to ditch the truck ASAP," Spivka said. "There's no way we'll make it to the salvage yard. They'll be looking for us. We've got to lose the truck, steal a car somewhere, and get the hell out of here. Once we get wheels, we can meet Harrington as planned and find out what the hell happened."

"You think any of those guys could ID us?"

"I hope not. But it's possible. We'll just have to take our chances and hope for the best. It's not good."

"What do we do with him?" Andrews said, gesturing toward Dimase.

"He doesn't look too good. What did you do to him?"

"I jabbed him with the syringe," Andrews replied. He looked at Dimase. "I don't think he's going to make it. We can't take him with us if we jack a car. Let's just leave him with the truck. If the stuff was going to kill Sumner, it should probably kill this guy too. He's the least of our worries right now."

Ten minutes later, Andrews pulled the truck into the large open parking lot at Tyson's Galleria. He did a quick survey for security cameras and parked as far away from them as he could, realizing he and Spivka would still be caught on tape. "Keep your hat and sunglasses on," he said. "Head down, and face away from the cameras as much as possible. Let's not give them anything to look at. Give me a hand. Let's lay this guy in the back of the truck."

They maneuvered Dimase into the back of the truck and lay him on his back. Dimase stared up at them with his eyes wide open but otherwise unable to move.

"All right," Spivka said. "Let's find a car and get outta Dodge."

CHAPTER 36

Sumner Residence, Forest Hills, Washington, DC

During the attack on Sumner's decoy, Ben Johnson, Harris Sumner, and two of Dimase's men were holed up in an upstairs bedroom. Dimase's men were armed and ready in case any attackers breached the homestead and made it inside the house.

Sumner remained uncertain how to interpret what was going on around him. They had come for him after midnight, kidnapping him and taking him hostage in his own house. Led by Dimase, an undercover team had gained entry to the Sumner residence and awakened the groggy justice in his bed. When he'd awakened, several armed men had surrounded his bed. One of them was holding the panic button that was normally kept on the nightstand. Sumner's security system had also been disabled. Summoning the Secret Service was not an option.

No one laid a hand on the justice, but they were positioned in such a way as to prevent him from making a wild dash or attempting to leave the bed. Dimase was closest to Sumner, and he repeatedly alternated between making the universal sign for silence by putting his index finger to his lips and making a calming gesture by gently motioning in a downward direction with the palms of his hands.

When the initial shock wore off, Sumner asked, "Who are you? What do you want?"

"We are here to help you," Dimase replied. "We will not hurt you."

"Why would I want your help? I don't believe you. I insist we call the Secret Service right away. They can protect me. You have no right to break into my house."

"We can't do that," Dimase said, and he went on to explain a thumbnail sketch of Operation SCOTUS.

When Dimase was finished, a skeptical Sumner said, "You are telling me the Secret Service is compromised? That's hard to believe."

"We don't know that for a fact," Dimase replied, "but we are certain the FBI has been compromised at the highest levels. It could extend to the Secret Service; we just don't know. Even if the Secret Service is clean, as a matter of protocol, they would bring the FBI into the loop, and we would lose our advantage. The bad guys within the FBI would know we were onto them and would change their plans. They would come after you some other time in some other way, and we wouldn't be able to protect you."

Sumner remained doubtful, but he had no choice at the moment except to remain compliant. Surely, he realized, if the men had wanted to kill him, they would already have done so, but the story of corrupt senators and rogue FBI agents was too tough to stomach, especially the fact that they wanted him dead.

Dimase continued to try to win Justice Sumner's confidence. "None of us have masks. We are not trying to hide our identities from you. We have not harmed you. I brought someone with me to show that you can believe us."

Ben Johnson stepped forward. "It's been many years, Justice Sumner, but we met at a charitable dinner for the Wounded Warriors Foundation. You were an up-and-coming district judge, and I run Fischer, Forbes, and Johnson." Ben stuck out his hand, and Sumner shook it.

"Yes, I remember you, and I've seen you in the news from time to time. What are you doing here?"

"It's a long story," Ben said, "but I'm an old friend of Dimase Augustin here, and he was working on something unrelated for me, when he stumbled into all this. He asked me to come tonight because he thought my presence might help provide some reassurance and credibility."

Sumner relaxed somewhat, and Dimase explained the plan to have a decoy take Sumner's place for his morning run. Ben and two men remained in the bedroom with Sumner while Dimase and the other operatives took up positions outside the house. The decoy stayed behind and put on a pair of gym shorts and a Georgetown University hoodie, ready to assume his role in the morning.

It was a long, tense night that passed mostly in silence and darkness. At 5:30 a.m., the decoy notified them that he was about to leave. They heard the front door close as the imposter left the house and then nothing for a full twenty-five minutes. Suddenly, they heard Dimase's voice through their earbuds, urgently yelling, "Go, go, go!" followed by several gunshots. The early dawn light filtered through the bedroom curtains, providing dim illumination. Sumner's eyes were wide with concern. Ben was nervous as well but trusted that the armed operatives next to him could handle anyone coming up the stairs. His greater worry was for the men downstairs, who apparently were involved in a firefight.

After a lengthy pause in the gunfire, Ben pulled the edge of the curtain slightly aside and sneaked a peek outside. What he saw shocked him: two men in UPS uniforms, with pistols drawn, were positioned back to back, holding Dimase between them and working their way down the driveway toward a UPS truck. Below, on the front porch, Ben could see the bodies of three of Dimase's men and the decoy lying as still as logs. There was nothing he could do except inform the others in the room. They had to hold their position to protect Sumner. There was no way to know the condition of Dimase's remaining men outside the house, but Ben assumed they had probably taken positions at the side of the house and were holding their fire to avoid hitting Dimase.

Ben continued watching through the slit in the curtain, providing a running narrative for the others. The two UPS figures made it to the far side of the truck, clutching Dimase tightly the entire time. They passed from Ben's view when they went around the truck, and within moments, the truck sped off. They had taken Dimase with them.

As soon as the truck was out of the sight, Dimase's two remaining operatives raced from each corner of the house to check on their fallen comrades.

"Stay with Sumner!" Ben shouted as he ran down the stairs to assess the situation himself.

On the porch, the three men who'd been shot were starting to stir. Each had been shot point-blank, center mass, but each was wearing a Kevlar vest. They were bruised and in shock but ultimately would be okay. Thankfully, the shooter had not opted for head shots.

Ben breathed a sigh of relief, but it was short-lived, as his focus returned to Dimase. "We've got to bring in the authorities now," he said. "We have no choice. We have to find that truck. It's the only way. Do you think the area is clear?"

"I think so," one of the operatives replied. "There were two of them."

"Okay, just to be safe, let's get everyone inside. Let's have Sumner call the Secret Service. When he tells them he's been attacked, that will trigger what we need."

Within minutes, a Secret Service team arrived to take Sumner into protective custody. An all-out search was launched for the UPS truck. Ben Johnson explained the urgency of finding Dimase, who had been held hostage and kidnapped. He also explained that the FBI had been compromised. After a lengthy discussion, with Sumner's strong influence, the Secret Service agent in charge agreed to keep the FBI out of the loop for the time being. To mobilize a maximum search effort, an altered all-points bulletin, or APB, was put out to all levels of law enforcement that a Secret Service agent was down and that a brown UPS box truck was wanted in connection with the attack.

Ben decided to hold back on mentioning Harrington in the discussion. There was no way to tell how many corrupt agents

Harrington controlled. Putting Harrington's name out there would have alerted any bad guys that they were possibly exposed, which might have resulted in unintended consequences. For now, they would quietly try to figure out where Harrington was but hold off on including him in the all-out manhunt.

State troopers and local law enforcement had a mandate to stop and search every UPS truck. Extreme caution was urged, as the suspects—two white males last seen wearing UPS uniforms—were considered armed and extremely dangerous. Security cameras on major highways were used to monitor and check every main artery emanating from the DC area, and a fleet of helicopters were dispatched to cover secondary roads. Roadblocks were also set up. A net was cast over the entire Washington, DC, area in the hope that they were not too late to snare the fake UPS truck.

Two hours passed, and still there was no sign of the truck or the two suspects. The control center for the search was set up at Secret Service headquarters. The FBI was brought into the loop, but the true identity of the suspects as FBI agents and the corruption of the FBI were not disclosed. They had to use the resources of the FBI without giving up the knowledge that they were aware of possible corruption within the agency. They could trust no one, but under the circumstances, any tainted bureau personnel would have to fully cooperate with the search effort or risk calling attention to themselves.

The Secret Service agent in charge was Tony Antonellis. "You and you two," he said, pointing to Ben and the two uninjured operatives from Dimase's unit. "Come back to the control center in order to provide any additional intelligence and background." He paused and then added to Ben, who was hesitant, "It's not much of a request."

"Let me make a phone call on the way," Ben said. He called Bill Larson, who, when he heard that Dimase had been kidnapped, took the first flight from Boston to DC and joined the others at Secret Service headquarters.

CHAPTER 37

Winchester, Virginia

Frank Harrington sat on a stool behind the counter in the manager's office at Dahl's Salvage and Scrap Metal. Dahl was stuffed in a back closet with a bullet in his head. The office was cluttered with an accumulation of debris, odd parts, pieces of metal stacked on steel shelving, and towering piles of paperwork and files. Apparently, Dahl hadn't believed in spending money on filing cabinets.

The bulletin board was overflowing with notices, work orders, and various flyers, all thumbtacked one over another. A three-year-old calendar featuring pictures of naked girls in various poses on different types of trucks hung on the wall behind the counter. The smell of diesel oil and cigar smoke hung in the air.

Harrington checked the time. If all had gone well, he knew Andrews and Spivka should be arriving in the UPS truck fairly soon. He dared not call or text them, in case things had gone wrong and someone other than Andrews and Spivka now had possession of their phones. Harrington had been careful to keep himself insulated from the physical execution of the mission, and the last thing he wanted to risk was electronic proof of communication between himself and

Andrews and Spivka at the time of the operation. Harrington wanted complete deniability and a solid alibi if he were ever questioned in connection with the plot.

There was no need for him to personally supervise or be anywhere near the scene. Andrews and Spivka were pros. Unless Harrington joined them as part of the assault team, which he had no intention of doing, there was nothing he could do from an observation post to influence the outcome one way or the other. Instead, he'd made sure that at the exact time of the attack, at least a dozen people had seen him having an early breakfast at a truck stop forty miles away.

Andrews and Spivka could sink or swim on their own. Harrington had his own plans. There was no turning back now.

A surreal calm had descended over Harrington. All the stress and anxiety were finally coming to an end. In the next twenty-four hours, either he would be safely away, or he would be dead. Strangely, he was okay with either outcome. He just wanted the insanity to be over. He would be at peace either way.

In his briefcase below the counter were a ticket to Mexico City and a fake passport under a false name. He'd acquired the passport at Quantico, and shortly after the fact, when all the shit hit the fan, the FBI would quickly figure out he'd used an identity created by undercover operations to flee the country. The FBI wouldn't know, however, that months earlier, Harrington had used the deep net to go online and create third and fourth identities and passports. Once he was safely in Mexico, he would simply vanish, and Frank Harrington, deputy assistant director of the FBI, would be no more.

He'd always heard Ecuador was nice. If everything fell into place, that was where he would begin his new life. One could buy a lot of privacy in Ecuador for $4 million. Of course, to reach that number and secure any loose ends, there was still work to do.

Harrington ran through the numbers in his head. He already had access to $1.5 million built up over time in his offshore accounts. Andrews and Spivka were owed another $375,000 each from what was left of the operating budget, but the big prize was the $2 million bonus that Monroe had promised him upon the successful completion of Operation SCOTUS. It was imperative that he see Monroe that day, collect the bonus, and get out of town.

Harrington checked his watch again. Andrews and Spivka were running a little late. The plan called for them to get the fake UPS truck to the salvage yard by 7:30 a.m., before the business opened for the day. Ideally, by the time the business opened at 8:30 a.m., the truck would no longer exist, and they would be long gone.

Of course, he had modified that plan, but Andrews and Spivka were in the dark with respect to any revisions. He would bring them up to speed soon enough. From Harrington's new viewpoint, it didn't really matter whether they had been successful in taking out Sumner. What mattered was that he kept his rendezvous with the two agents and then saw Monroe before any news of the morning's events reached him.

Until the attack on Sumner hit the news, Harrington was the only conduit through which Monroe would learn the outcome of the operation. The timing was critical because by late morning, there were sure to be news reports about whatever had gone down with Sumner. It didn't matter what had actually happened. For Harrington to get the $2 million bonus transferred to his account, Monroe had to believe the operation was successful. Once that window passed, Harrington would be home free. Only Monroe had the transfer codes. Only Monroe could execute the transaction. For that to occur, Monroe would have to believe Operation SCOTUS had been successful.

Harrington heard the sound of a vehicle pull up and park outside the office. Strangely, the engine sounded too small to be that of a truck. He came from behind the counter, crossed the room to look out a window, and was surprised to see Andrews and Spivka emerge from a late-model sedan. Neither of them looked happy. Harrington opened the office door as they approached. "What happened?" he asked. "Where's the truck?"

"We ditched it," Spivka said. "We left it in a parking lot and left a body in the back."

Harrington was surprised. "A body in the back? Who?"

"No idea," Andrews said. "The operation was a bust. We were set up. They were waiting for us."

Again, Harrington was surprised. "How did it go down?"

"They had a decoy for Sumner!" Spivka yelled. "We never saw Sumner. A guy came out of the house at the expected time, stretched out, and took off on his run. From our distance, we just assumed it was Sumner. I mean, he had a hoodie on, but who else would it have been? When he left, we moved up as planned. When he returned, we timed everything perfectly, but right as I got close, he attacked me. That was when I realized it wasn't Sumner. Then all hell broke loose—guys came running out of nowhere, and we barely fought our way out."

"Who's the dead guy in the truck?" Harrington asked again. "Where'd he come from?"

"During the fight, I stuck him in the neck with the hypo. Spiv and I formed up back to back and used the guy as a shield to work our way back to the truck. Whatever stuff was in the needle, it worked. The guy was stiff as a board within five minutes. We figured they'd put an APB out on the truck way before we'd have time to get here, so we dumped it and stole a car. The stiff is still in the back of the truck."

"Unbelievable," Harrington said. "I wonder how the hell they knew we were coming."

"I don't know," Andrews said, "but I don't have a good feeling about it. If those guys ID us as FBI, we're finished."

"There's something funny about that," Spivka said. "I think there were only six of them. If Secret Service got wind of the operation, wouldn't you expect a whole lot more than that? And tons of other assets ready to move in and create a perimeter? We would never have gotten away if they'd done that. I don't think these guys were government. It's almost as if they were private security or something like that."

Harrington was not concerned about whether Andrewes and Spivka had been identified or had left any evidence in the UPS truck. By the time the day was over, it would be obvious the two FBI agents were the assailants who'd carried out the attack at Sumner's residence. His main concern at the moment was wrapping things up there and getting to Monroe as soon as possible before word of the mission's failure spread any further.

"Look," Harrington said with feigned concern, "we'll regroup eventually and figure out what happened. For now, I want you guys to have what's coming to you out of the operations budget. You need to lay low for a while. This will tide you over, and if you do have to run, you'll have enough money to disappear."

Andrews and Spivka followed Harrington back behind the counter, where Harrington picked up the briefcase. He removed a laptop and tapped a few keys. "Here." He grinned. "Don't ever say we don't reward loyalty. Watch—you can see the transfer and confirm it for yourselves."

Both agents leaned in to look at the computer screen. Harrington stepped back, subtly creating space. Before either man could react, Harrington drew his service revolver from the holster at the small of his back and, in rapid succession, placed a single bullet at the base of each agent's skull.

Andrews and Spivka slumped forward over the counter and then slowly collapsed to the floor. A patina of blood and brains covered the countertop where they had been standing. Harrington closed his laptop and put it back in the briefcase. He exited the office and jumped into his FBI SUV. The Escalade's engine roared to life, and he drove from the salvage yard in a hurry. He had to get to Dick Monroe as soon as possible to inform the senator about the successful completion of Operation SCOTUS.

◆　◆　◆

Secret Service Headquarters, Washington, DC

The first break came when local police called in a triple murder at a place called Dahl's Salvage and Scrap Metal in rural Culpepper County in northeastern Virginia. Two of the dead guys were wearing UPS uniforms, but there was no sign of the truck. The responding officers were aware of the APB on the UPS truck and assumed the victims were the probable suspects of the massive search. Secret Service, FBI, and state police swarmed the scene, searching the entire property, but there was still no clue as to the whereabouts of Dimase or the missing truck.

The victim shot in the head and stuffed in a closet was quickly identified as George Dahl, the proprietor of the salvage yard. The other two victims had no identifying documents on their persons. Ben, Bill Larson, and the Secret Service agent in charge, Tony Antonellis, assumed it was highly probable the two men were rogue FBI agents. With the aid of facial-recognition software and with confirmation by the process of elimination and wellness checks, they soon identified the two remaining victims as Andrews and Spivka, both active FBI agents. The news sent a ripple through the control room, particularly surprising the FBI liaison who was channeling instructions to agents in the field and coordinating with his superiors at Quantico.

Ben Johnson and Bill Larson held a quick side conference with each other. Until then, they had not mentioned that they suspected Harrington of pulling the trigger in the murder of Rufus Manteau's FBI handler in Alexandria. It was one thing to suggest there were dirty FBI agents involved in a plot to assassinate a Supreme Court justice; it was even worse to accuse the number-three man at the FBI of killing fellow agents. Unsure whom to trust, they had kept the knowledge to themselves to that point.

"It has to be Harrington who killed those two guys. Don't you think?" Ben whispered.

"Yeah," Larson said. "I think it's time to tell them and get an APB out on him. He's trying to cover his tracks. He has to be the shooter at the salvage yard. He took those guys out the same way he took out the agent in Alexandria."

Ben was motioning Tony Antonellis over, when all of a sudden, there was a shout from across the room. "We've found the truck!" an agent exclaimed. "It's parked at Tyson's Galleria. Mall security spotted it and notified the staties, who notified us. There's a guy in the back of the truck."

"It has to be Dimase," Ben said excitedly. "Is he alive?"

"Alive but unresponsive," the agent said. "An ambulance and EMTs are on the scene. He's about to be transported to Inova Fairfax Hospital."

CHAPTER 38

Watergate Apartments, Washington, DC

Harrington parked the Escalade around the corner from the Watergate and made his way on foot to the lobby. He'd given it some thought and decided it would be best not to call ahead. Instead, he wanted to drop in on Monroe unannounced. As he had serious doubts about the senator's reliability, his judgment was to use the element of surprise to his advantage and attempt to get the drop on Monroe.

Given Harrington's timetable for getting out of the country, it wouldn't matter if he was recognized in the lobby or on security cameras. He had already committed several felonies that would be easily tied to him. As long as he had enough time to disappear, none of that would matter. It was critical that he get in, get paid, and get out.

Harrington was fairly certain the senator would be in his apartment. If not, he'd have to improvise on the fly. Hopefully, by his skipping the advanced phone call, Monroe wouldn't be expecting him just yet.

If Harrington was correct and Monroe viewed him as expendable once Operation SCOTUS was completed, there was no way Monroe would willingly pay the $2 million bonus. He doubted Monroe would try to take him out in his own apartment, and he didn't think Monroe would attempt the act himself; nonetheless, he had to be ready for anything.

Harrington exited the elevator on Monroe's floor and lingered in the hallway. He was hoping he might bump into a maid and use his FBI badge to convince her to let him into Monroe's unit. After five minutes, there was no sign of a maid, but an elderly woman left her apartment and walked toward the elevator. "Excuse me," Harrington said. "Could you please do me a huge favor? I'm locked out of my unit. Would you mind calling housekeeping so they can send someone by?" He flashed his most engaging smile. He was dressed in a suit and looked as if he belonged.

After a brief pause, the woman smiled back. "Of course. Let me step back into my unit and use the house phone. I'll be right back."

"Thank you," Harrington said. "I'll wait here. I appreciate it."

A few moments later, the woman returned. "They are on their way up," she said reassuringly as she pushed the elevator call button.

"Thanks again," Harrington called as the elevator doors closed behind her.

Within minutes, a maid appeared, and Harrington signaled her over. He assumed she probably had a pretty good idea of who lived in which unit, so he decided not to pretend to be a tenant and instead waved his FBI badge at her. "I have to ask you to let me into this apartment," he said, standing outside Monroe's door. "Quietly, please."

The maid looked hesitant, so Harrington bent in close with his face inches from hers. "This is a matter of national security. Open the door now, or I'll have you arrested."

The maid reached inside the pocket of her smock and pulled out a plastic key card. Harrington took the card himself, quietly unlocked the door, and cracked it slightly, looking inside. Seeing no immediate threat, he returned the card to the maid. "Forget you ever saw me here, unless you want a boatload of trouble." He shooed her away and entered the apartment, gently closing the door behind him.

Harrington stood frozen just inside the entrance, listening intently for any sound. He heard a faint hum of running water from somewhere within and advanced a little farther. The sound was coming from the master bedroom at the end of a short hallway. Harrington paused again outside the closed bedroom door. It sounded like Monroe was in the shower, which was a stroke of luck. He entered the bedroom. A pair of slacks, a dress shirt, and underwear were laid out at the foot of the king-sized bed. Harrington scooted across the room and positioned himself in the master closet, pulling the louvered double doors closed behind him. He drew his service revolver and held it at the ready, listening for the water to stop.

When the shower shut off, he heard Monroe move around in the bathroom and then come into the bedroom. Monroe was humming softly to himself. Harrington cracked the closet doors enough to see Monroe at the foot of the bed, naked and toweling himself off. He had his back to Harrington with one foot on the bed, drying his leg.

Harrington moved like a cat, crossing the room in an instant and pressing the muzzle of his weapon into his back.

Monroe didn't turn around but stood up straight. "Frank, is that you?" he asked with calmness. "I thought you were going to call first. Was the operation a success?"

"Yes, Dick, a major success," Harrington lied. "Sumner is gone. Everything went off without a hitch, exactly as planned."

"Excellent," Monroe said despite the gun poking into his ribs, with his hands slightly raised and still facing away. "So why the dramatic entrance and the gun to my back?"

"Just being cautious. Some of the things you've said and done lately have not exactly inspired my confidence. I thought perhaps now that Operation SCOTUS is done, you might find me expendable—you know, a loose end."

"Nonsense," Monroe replied. "I need you. You know that. I said those things in the heat of the moment. You and I are a team, Frank."

"Yes, well, that may be, but I resign, and I want to get paid before I leave."

"What are you talking about?" Monroe said. "Why would you leave now, when we are on the cusp of accomplishing what we set out to do? We've done it, Frank. Don't you see?"

"I see all right. I see that you could just as easily do without me—you know, like my man in Alexandria. No, Dick, I've had enough. I'm going to disappear. You can find someone to take my place. I don't care about grand schemes or visions of power. Four million dollars is more than enough for me. I'm out."

"Okay, have it your way, but you're making a big mistake. I would have always taken care of you."

"Let's just take a walk into the other room, fire up that computer, and pay me so I can be on my way."

"Okay," Monroe said as he wrapped the towel around his waist. The two men proceeded to a spare bedroom that Monroe used as an office. Monroe sat at the desk and turned on the computer. "You certainly earned your bonus, Frank. Are you sure I can't talk you out of leaving?"

"Just make the transfer. I'm in a bit of a hurry," Harrington said, nudging Monroe with the muzzle of the firearm. With his free hand, he pulled out his cell phone and brought up an app with a summary of his offshore accounts. "Go ahead. I've got my accounts up on my phone. I'll be able to confirm when the funds are received. Two million, as agreed."

Given no choice, Monroe spent a full two minutes tapping various keys and finally hit a button to execute the transfer. Harrington watched over his shoulder as the funds moved from one account to the other; a green bar spread across the screen indicated the percentage completed as the funds moved. When the green bar filled to 100 percent, Harrington checked his phone and confirmed that all $2 million had been received.

"Thank you, Senator. Now I need to ask you one last favor. I need your driver to drop me at the airport. I have a flight to catch, and I'd rather not use my own car to get there."

"What's wrong with your own car?" Monroe asked.

"Let's just say I want to get a head start on getting out of the country, and I don't want to leave my car at the airport as a clue that I flew out. I'd rather they take a few days to figure out where I went and how I got there."

"Okay. You're sure I can't talk you out of this? Where will you go?"

"Quite sure, Dick. I was thinking South America is pretty nice. They say Americans are treated very well in Ecuador. Now, call your driver, and order him to pick me up out front in fifteen minutes."

Recognizing that he had little choice, Monroe made the call. "Now what?" he asked afterward.

"Now I'll be saying goodbye," Harrington replied. He reached into his pocket and withdrew the extra hypodermic of succinylcholine he'd brought for the occasion. Originally, he'd thought he might be able to use the drug on Monroe to make his death look like a heart attack in much the same way they had intended to use it on Justice Sumner. Now it was obvious the murder would eventually be traced back to him. The maid would break down under questioning and say she had let him into Monroe's apartment. He would have been caught on security cameras in the lobby and in the hallway by Monroe's unit. The driver would testify that he'd picked up Harrington and driven him to the airport. All the other murders and crimes he'd committed would soon be out in the open.

None of that mattered at the moment. There was a certain satisfying sense of justice in using succinylcholine on Monroe. *What goes around comes around*, he thought. Also, having Monroe's death initially look like a suicide would confuse things and give Harrington a little more time to disappear before his former colleagues pieced everything together.

Harrington plunged the needle into the side of Monroe's neck and released the full load of succinylcholine. Still seated, Monroe instinctively reached for his neck and then rose weakly to his feet. "What have you done?" he stammered, starting to go into shock.

"Just cleaning up a few loose ends," Harrington replied. "I'm sure you understand."

Monroe tried to strike out, but already he was losing muscle control. He staggered across the room as Harrington easily backpedaled, staying just out of his reach. The dose Harrington had administered was four times what would have been called for in a normal surgical procedure. As the drug took effect, Monroe would remain fully conscious, but all his muscles would quickly become paralyzed.

Harrington watched as Monroe stumbled about the room and finally collapsed to the floor. Monroe's eyes were wide open with terror as he lay on the floor, unable to move, staring up at his attacker. Harrington prodded him with his foot to make sure his victim was completely incapacitated. When he was fully satisfied, he went back to Monroe's bedroom and returned with two belts he'd found hanging from a rack in the closet. He dragged Monroe's rigid body into the living room, where he looped one belt around the senator's neck and positioned him on the floor beneath a large ceiling fan. Monroe was unable to speak or react in any way. Only his eyes gave away the horror of his situation.

Harrington dragged two hard-backed chairs from the dining room table and placed them under the fan. He looped the second belt around the base of the ceiling fixture and then tied off the other end through the belt around Monroe's neck. Monroe was a dead weight, but standing on the adjacent chair, Harrington managed to maneuver and support him into an upright position on the chair directly beneath the fan. Monroe stared helplessly straight ahead. Harrington looked Monroe in the eye and, with a wink and a nod to his former colleague, pulled the chair from beneath Monroe's feet.

The body immediately dropped about eight inches, but there was little twitching or convulsing; every muscle was frozen in paralysis from the megadose of succinylcholine. Harrington returned the second chair to the dining room, and on his way out, he couldn't resist flicking the switch to turn on the fan. So much for making it look like a suicide. Monroe's body shot up as the belt wrapped around the fan before jamming it in place. Monroe's neck was stuck at an awkward, impossible angle, and his lifeless eyes still stared straight ahead, now dull with death.

As he exited the apartment, Harrington shut off the lights. By then, Monroe's limo driver would be waiting out front. It was time to catch a flight to a new life.

CHAPTER 39

Secret Service Headquarters, Washington, DC

Before Ben and Bill Larson asked permission to go to the hospital to check on Dimase, they called over Tony Antonellis and told him why they thought Harrington had been the shooter at the salvage yard. When they were finished, Antonellis was incredulous.

"You are telling me that the number-three guy in the FBI actually flew to Louisiana and killed one of his own agents, and now he's killed two more agents at the salvage yard? This guy is a piece of work. Do you think it's time to put an APB out on him?"

Larson thought about that for a moment. "The downside to putting out an APB is that it lets the cat out of the bag. If there are other bad agents out there, once they know we're looking for Harrington and that this is not just about searching for a UPS truck involved with a downed Secret Service agent, they'll shift into cover-up mode, and we may never know who they are."

"True," Antonellis replied. "If we hold back a bit longer about what's really going on, Harrington might lead us to others in his network. For that to happen, we have to figure out where he is first."

"Why don't you try to contact him through routine FBI channels to see if he responds? Send a couple Secret Service guys to his house, and see what they can find. Keep it on the down low for now. Maybe he'll pick up the phone if someone calls him on a routine matter. If he doesn't think we're onto him yet, he might try to bluff his way through any conversation in order to buy extra time for whatever he's up to next."

Antonellis agreed.

Two hours later, Ben and Larson were bedside with their colleague at Inova Fairfax Hospital. Dimase looked like he'd been through the ringer, but he smiled weakly at them through an array of tubes and wires. He was starting to regain muscle movement after the doctors had administered an antidote to the succinylcholine. Dimase was fortunate. Apparently, the needle had broken off in his neck, and he had received only a portion of the megadose in the hypodermic. If he'd gotten the full dose, he would no longer have been among the living. As it was, they planned to keep him overnight in the hospital. Doctors believed that by the following day, he would be pretty much back to normal.

Once Ben and Larson were assured that Dimase would be okay, the conversation turned to Operation SCOTUS. Ben brought Dimase up to date on the salvage yard murders and the decision not to put out an APB on Harrington yet.

"What about Monroe?" Dimase asked. "Is anyone keeping tabs on him?"

"We didn't bring him into it yet," Larson replied. "Everything was moving so fast. It's only been a few hours since the attack. We didn't see Monroe as an immediate physical threat. There'll be plenty of time later to investigate how widespread the conspiracy is. When Justice Sumner called the Secret Service, he told them what we had told him— that there was a plot to take him out and that it might involve rogue FBI agents and possibly other levels of law enforcement. The priority was to protect him after the attack. If you start making accusations beyond the immediate attackers at this stage of the game, against senators or high-ranking FBI officials, you don't know what you're going to trigger. We figured we should contain the threat and then reassess in the aftermath. This mess is a whole lot more complicated than a simple murder. There are all kinds of political and even national security implications. If we are premature on going after the guys at the top, they will just cover up and lawyer up, and we'll never know how far-reaching the corruption is. We are talking about a possible plot to take down the government of the United States. There's no telling how far it goes and who's involved, so we held off for now."

"That makes sense," Dimase said. "Now that Sumner is safe, maybe the best thing for us to do with our own people is to refocus on Harrington and Monroe. If anything develops, we can bring in the Secret Service. We still have bugs in Monroe's Watergate apartment, right? What's the latest report on those?"

"The recordings are voice-activated. When we shifted our resources to protecting Sumner, I had the monitoring feed rerouted to our Boston office with instructions to check for activity every six hours. You want to do an interim check-in with them to see if anything got caught on tape so far today?"

Dimase nodded, and Larson put his cell phone on speaker mode to call Boston. The operative in their Boston office relayed that there had been no activity on his last check but said he would listen to see if anything had occurred since then. "The digital recording only lasts as long as there is sound to be picked up." The man put the phone on hold for a couple minutes and then came back on the line. "There's twelve minutes on there," he said excitedly. "That's over a five-hour period since my last check."

"Put it on the speaker, and play it from the beginning for all of us," Dimase said.

The first sound they heard was of muffled voices. It was impossible to distinguish individual words, but the tone sounded conversational.

"It sounds like two people," Dimase said. "They must be in one of the bedrooms. The bugs are only in the living room and kitchen. Play the beginning back again."

They all strained to try to make out the conversation, but the words were unintelligible. They continued playing the tape. After three or four minutes, the tone changed somewhat. At least one of the parties raised his voice briefly in what sounded like a note of alarm. That was followed by a soft thud. The sound grew louder as someone apparently walked into one of the front rooms. They heard mild scraping and banging and then nothing.

"What do you think we just listened to?" Ben asked.

"I don't know, but I think we'd better get someone over there," Dimase replied. "At first, there seemed to be two voices—then none. I wonder if Harrington paid Monroe a visit."

CHAPTER
40

Watergate Complex

Harrington strode as casually as he could through the lobby and out the front entrance of the building. He looked left and right, but Monroe's limo driver was nowhere to be found. He thought back to the call Monroe had made with the gun stuck in his ribs. *Son of a bitch. How could I be so stupid?*

Harrington, of all people, should have anticipated the technique. It was security training 101. Monroe had used code words to alert his driver that he was in danger. Police were probably on their way to the scene at that moment.

The aura of calm that had enveloped Harrington over the past twenty-four hours dissipated instantly. The shakes returned, and his breathing grew rapid and shallow. He looked at his watch but couldn't read the numbers. They seemed to vibrate back and forth in a rapid blur.

He had to get to the airport, and he had to do it fast. He dared not take his own Escalade. He tried to calculate backward from his flight's scheduled departure time to the present moment, filling in the sequence and timing of how and when law enforcement would unravel what had happened and identify him. Of course, they would immediately put out an APB, blanketing the city in an all-out manhunt. The murder of a sitting US senator was about as big a deal as there could be.

He had made no great effort to avoid being seen on his way up to Monroe's apartment. In his mind, it wasn't a matter of whether the authorities would link him to Monroe's bizarre death after finding him hanging from a ceiling fan in his living room; it was a matter of how quickly they would do it. He had planned on being well away when that happened; now that was far from certain.

He looked at the short line of cabs in front of the Watergate and headed toward them. As he approached, the first cab in line took off, apparently with a fare already inside. The second cab rolled up to the head of the queue, and a young woman stepped forward and opened the rear door, mere feet ahead of Harrington.

His fingers and the forearm muscles on his left arm began twitching uncontrollably as anxiety threatened once again to overtake him. He thrust his hand into his pants pocket to prevent anyone from noticing and looked expectantly at the next taxi in line, but the first cab had yet to budge, locking the others in place. Through the windows, Harrington could see the woman and the cab driver having an animated discussion.

Suddenly, from around the corner, a police squad car burst into the Watergate driveway. Within seconds, two more squad cars arrived with lights flashing and sirens blaring. Harrington looked back at the first cab, which still had not moved. In a panic, he pulled open the door to the second cab in line and jumped into the backseat. The surprised cabbie looked at him in the rearview mirror.

"Get me to the airport," Harrington blurted out.

"Okay," the driver replied, but he didn't put the car in gear.

"Now." Harrington gulped. "I've got to catch a flight. Please. Let's go."

"I can't go until he goes," the cabbie said, gesturing toward the first cab.

"Just pull around him," Harrington said.

"I can't," the man replied. "What if the lady jumps out again? I'll get in trouble. Besides, he's my friend. I can't steal his fare."

"For the love of God, man!" Harrington screamed, about to lose it. "I can't miss that flight!" He pulled two hundred-dollar bills from his wallet and held them up to the Plexiglas separating him from the driver. The man flashed a toothy grin and slid the partition aside in order to accept the cash.

"You talked me into it," the cabbie said.

Harrington slumped back in his seat. As they exited the driveway and the taxi accelerated down Virginia Avenue, Harrington saw three additional police cars racing in the opposite direction toward the Watergate.

He unbuttoned the top button of his shirt. There was still one more problem: he had to retrieve his carry-on from the Escalade. Everything he needed to change identities was in the false bottom of that luggage. He banged his fist on the Plexiglas to get the driver's attention. "Take the next right!" he shouted through the circle of small holes designed to let the driver communicate with passengers.

"I thought you wanted to go to the airport!" the cabbie yelled back.

"I do. One quick stop first. Now! Do it!"

The cabbie twisted the wheel, and the car made a sharp turn at the last moment.

"Down there!" Harrington shouted, pointing with his index finger, even though the driver wasn't looking at him. "Pull over at the end of the block."

The cabbie did as he was told, and Harrington leaped from the car almost before it had jolted to a stop. He fumbled for the key fob in his pocket and ran to the SUV. He shot a quick look back at the cab, afraid the man might just take off without him, but the taxi remained in place. Harrington hit the unlock button and grabbed the small suitcase on the floor in the backseat. He didn't bother to relock the Escalade as he hustled back to the cab. No matter what happened next, it was unlikely he would ever see the Cadillac again.

"What's going on?" the cabbie said.

"Airport!" Harrington screamed again. "Just get me to the airport."

The cabbie slid the partition back and turned to frame his face in the small opening. He smiled the smile of a street player who knew he had leverage. Harrington noticed that one of his front teeth was capped in gold.

"You think I'm stupid, man?" the cabbie said.

Harrington was tempted to take the pistol from his pocket and threaten to blow the man's fucking brains out, but he was still rational enough to realize that would seal his own doom in the end. He had to get on that plane. "How much?" he asked.

"Another two hundred," the cabbie replied.

Harrington forked over the money. "Go! Just go!"

By the time they arrived at Dulles International, Harrington felt as if he were going to jump out of his skin. He stuffed his pistol beneath the driver's seat, exited the cab, and clutched the carry-on as he headed straight for TSA. A state trooper glanced in his direction but then looked away.

Inside the terminal, Harrington felt as if everyone were looking at him, particularly anyone in uniform. The thought struck him that he probably should be more worried about those not in uniform. The airport would be full of undercover personnel from various agencies. He had to blend in. He had to get on board that plane before anyone noticed him.

Harrington hadn't planned on using any disguise during the first leg of his journey to Mexico City, just the first of the fake passports. There was no option to employ much of a disguise now. To soothe his nerves more than for any practical advantage, he stopped in a gift store and bought a Washington Nationals cap and a Georgetown University sweatshirt. He ducked into the nearest men's room, ditched his sport coat, and donned the new apparel.

Rather than using his own precheck TSA ID to get through security, he opted for his new temporary name and fake passport. The TSA line was long and moved slowly. When at last it was his turn, he placed his small suitcase on the x-ray machine conveyor belt, along with the few items on his person, and passed through the scanner. The alarm went off, and a large, bored-looking male TSA officer asked him to repeat the process.

Again, the alarm went off. *Damn hip replacement,* Harrington thought. He had forgotten all about it because it had been so long since he'd had to go through standard security.

"Please step over here, sir," the officer said, passing him off to another uniformed agent, who was holding a wand.

"It's my hip," Harrington stammered. "I had it replaced five years ago."

"No worries," the officer with the wand said. "Please hold your arms out like this." The man went on to describe what he was going to do and where he would be touching Harrington. Despite the relatively cool temperature in the terminal, Harrington could feel perspiration dripping down the back of his neck and collecting under his armpits.

"Are you feeling okay, sir?" the agent asked.

"Yes, yes, I just hate to fly, and I'm running late."

"Okay, you're all set," the agent said, waving him through.

In reality, Harrington still had two hours to kill before his flight boarded. He hadn't anticipated that events would unravel like this. Originally, he'd wanted to leave plenty of margin to finish his business with Monroe and safely get to the airport. Now time was his enemy.

Harrington wasn't worried that authorities would already be aware of his new identity. The bigger risk was that they would put out an APB on Frank Harrington and someone would recognize him. An APB would include extra coverage at both major DC airports as well as any other means of egress from the city via mass transportation.

There was only one way he could think of to stay completely out of sight: Frank Harrington spent the next two hours sitting fully clothed in a stall in the men's room.

◆　◆　◆

Bill Larson and Ben Johnson left Dimase at the hospital, promising to get back to him as soon as they checked out Monroe's apartment at the Watergate. On the way to the parking garage, Larson called Tony

Antonellis at the Secret Service, putting him on speakerphone. He informed Antonellis of the digital recording and suggested they were now at a point where the APB on Frank Harrington could not be held back any longer.

"You're too late," Antonellis said. "I put the APB out ten minutes ago. Monroe is dead, and Harrington is on the run."

Ben shook his head. "Knew it," he said softly.

"Good luck," Larson replied. "We had better find him before he kills anyone else."

◆　◆　◆

Congressman Francois LaFleur hung up his desk phone and stared at his brother, Alphonse, with an expression of shock on his face. "It's all coming apart," he said flatly. "We've got to protect ourselves."

"What happened?" Alphonse asked, rising from the soft leather chair by the coffee table. "What's wrong?"

"Monroe is dead. Killed in his apartment. There's an APB out on Frank Harrington. They think he did it."

"Frank Harrington of the FBI? I thought he was with us. Do we have any direct exposure? Have you met him in person?"

"Yeah, a couple times, but not about Operation SCOTUS. Maybe about some other stuff we wouldn't want to come out."

"What kind of stuff?" Alphonse asked, growing more concerned each moment.

"Mostly recruiting stuff—approaching other politicians, feeling them out, and pulling them into our network. Maybe some donors and corporate types as well."

"Yeah, well, I was around for most of that, Francois, and it had nothing to do directly with Harrington. I've never even met the guy."

"Phonse, don't you get it? Look two steps ahead for once. It's not what we did with Harrington; it's what he knows. He was Monroe's right hand. Operation SCOTUS was just the latest crazy scheme. Monroe was dirty for a long time. You and I were up to our necks in some of that stuff—kickbacks, extortion, illegal campaign contributions, money laundering. Even with Operation SCOTUS, we figured it out before the fact. None of that will play well if Harrington starts talking."

Alphonse started to pace back and forth with his hands thrust in his pants pockets. "What are we going to do?"

"I need you to make the rounds quietly. Start with our own staff. Purge everything. It's impossible to separate what might be incriminating from what's not. Destroy all cell phones, delete emails, and cleanse the files. I'd rather stonewall and plead ignorance than risk having the feds go on a fishing expedition through all that stuff."

"You think that will work? People talk."

"Do what you can to bottle it up. If people break ranks, it will be our word against theirs. We're in survival mode here. I'm not going to prison."

"What else?"

"When you're done with our own staff, go see the people we've done business with. Make it clear what the stakes are. If we go down, we are not going alone."

"What about Harrington?" Alphonse asked.

"Let's just pray he doesn't turn up anytime soon."

◆　◆　◆

Mexico City International Airport: Nine Hours Later

A couple thousand miles away, Frank Harrington once again stepped into a men's room stall for what he hoped would be the last time in a long time. Back in DC, he'd been able to board the plane without incident, appearing at the gate shortly before the plane's doors closed, limiting his window of visibility to less than two minutes. He hadn't relaxed until the wheels touched down in Mexico, but now he was feeling considerably more confident.

When he emerged minutes later, his identity had changed once again. Hopefully, for the rest of the world, that was where his trail would end. Harrington glanced in the mirror to double-check his blond wig and glue-on mustache, smiling at the image he saw. He headed to a ticket desk to buy round-trip tickets to Ecuador in order to enhance the deception. There would be no return trip. That day was the first day of the rest of his new life.

CHAPTER
41

Washington, DC: Six Months Later

Augustin and Larson LLC had turned over all the surveillance audio from Monroe's apartment to the Secret Service. The Secret Service, in turn, had brought in the CIA. Although the CIA was legally prohibited from operating on a domestic basis, the president, in an unprecedented use of the Emergency Powers Act, had issued a secret executive order authorizing the CIA to explicitly assist the Secret Service and the FBI in a complete and thorough investigation of Operation SCOTUS. The public was never to know how close the country had come to losing its most sacred and trusted institutions.

The CIA had been able to enhance the audiotape from Monroe's apartment and reconstruct most of the last conversation between Harrington and Monroe. The tape confirmed the extent of the corruption both men were involved in and Monroe's role at the top. It also confirmed that Harrington had murdered the FBI agent in Alexandria.

When Monroe had been found hanging from a ceiling fan in his apartment, the true nature of his death had been concealed. As far as the public was concerned, it had been a tragic suicide—a good man and public servant caught up in the depths of despair over some sort of personal issue.

Forensics eventually had confirmed that Harrington was also responsible for Monroe's murder and the three murders at the salvage yard, including two FBI agents. An interagency Internal Affairs investigation, in part based on the tree chart of Monroe's contacts developed by Augustin and Larson, had gathered enough evidence to indict ten FBI agents and force the resignation of several others. A number of politicians, bureaucrats, and political operatives also had been indicted or cast under suspicion.

In El Paso, Texas, Rufus Manteau finally had been arrested, and he was being held in federal custody pending prosecution. Manteau, when questioned extensively by the authorities, had corroborated the role of the dead FBI agent in Alexandria as his handler. Beyond that, his testimony was of little value. He had never heard of Harrington or Monroe, nor did he have a connection to any other corrupt agents.

Based largely on the evidence gathered by Dimase Augustin, Manteau eventually broke down and confessed to his role in the attack on Acadia LaFleur and the murder of Cady LaFleur, the hooker. In an effort to avoid the death penalty, he also agreed to a plea bargain and admitted to killing the victims at Cabrini Hospital, even though his guilt was somewhat of a foregone conclusion, given how visible he had been on the surveillance cameras.

The audiotape from Monroe's Watergate apartment also had yielded one other significant detail: Harrington clearly made a reference to South America, specifically Ecuador. Investigators had determined early on that Harrington had flown to Mexico City under an FBI alias. At that point, the trail had gone cold. However, once they'd enhanced the audiotape, the reference to Ecuador had become a key focus. The CIA had assets there.

Initially, there was no clue as to the identity Harrington might have assumed after Mexico City and whether he had actually gone on to Ecuador. The CIA, working with Mexican authorities, painstakingly reviewed flight manifests and passenger logs for the weeks after Harrington's arrival date in Mexico City. One by one, they eliminated possible suspects as they confirmed their identities. After weeks of effort, the search was finally narrowed to one man: an Irish businessman named Edmund Fahey, who was, in fact, actually Frank Harrington. Again, the trail dead-ended, this time in Ecuador. There was no trace of Edmund Fahey once he stepped off the plane at Marsical Sucre International Airport in Quito, Ecuador.

The president's secret executive order declared Harrington, a.k.a. Fahey, a threat to national security and designated Operation SCOTUS as a "clear and present danger to the security of the United States." The order provided the CIA with exceptional latitude in resolving the threat. Ecuador became the new focus of the investigation, with the CIA taking the lead. In a matter of that nature, the CIA was uniquely equipped to handle the issue in ways the FBI and Secret Service were not, particularly on foreign soil.

The president, through his people, made it clear that Harrington was not to be brought back to the United States for a public inquisition. There would be no show trial and no televised hearings. The conspiracy would end with Harrington. Public confidence in the institutions of the US government had to be maintained at all costs. There would be and could be no hint that a handful of men could corrupt the Supreme Court of the United States. The United States was not a banana republic.

Harrington had already disappeared. The CIA's mandate was to make sure he did not reappear—ever. As far as the public was concerned, the murders of the FBI agents in Alexandria and in Virginia had been part of a busted intelligence operation carried out by Russian agents. If any other details about Operation SCOTUS ever leaked out through the media, they would be explained away as being linked to the same Russian plot. The integrity of the Supreme Court would remain above reproach. Justice had been and would be served.

◆　◆　◆

Andean Foothills, Ecuador, South America

Frank Harrington sat alone on the expansive deck of his hacienda in the hills of eastern Ecuador. With the Andes Mountains as a backdrop, the view was spectacular, and he was finally at peace. It was like watching a wide-screen movie on the Travel Channel. The clear bright blue sky stretched to eternity. A light breeze roiled the long grass of the foothills, causing it to undulate and roll in sweeping waves, an ocean of green breaking upon the mountain shores.

Harrington was just reaching for his iced tea, when the movie went black. He never knew what happened as the sniper's bullet entered the front of his head and blew out the back of his skull. There was no fear or anticipation in advance and no pain or suffering after. In one nanosecond, the show simply stopped playing, and the theater went dark.

◆　◆　◆

United States Penitentiary, Atlanta, Georgia

Rufus Manteau lasted three months in federal prison before fate caught up to him in the form of double socks loaded with five-pound weights from the prison gymnasium. It was a tough way to go.

Unfortunately for Alphonse LaFleur, he was caught on a wire ordering the hit on Manteau and, as a result, faced twenty to life. In the aftermath of Operation SCOTUS, the scope of the joint investigative efforts of the FBI, Secret Service, and CIA was unprecedented. Dimase's original tree chart of Monroe's contacts had been expanded and leveraged to ensnare many others in the process. The intermediary Alphonse had used to set up the prison murder of Manteau had been turned and was cooperating with police in an effort to reduce his own sentence. Alphonse had no defense.

◆　◆　◆

Francois LaFleur was more fortunate. He had been smart enough and cold enough to leave the dirty work to his brother. The widespread federal probe into Operation SCOTUS had temporarily quashed much of the illegal or unethical activity throughout Washington. The swamp was in cover-up mode. Wide swaths of electronic and physical evidence were destroyed in offices across the city. An unlucky few were caught up in the investigation, but most just hunkered down.

When Harrington did not materialize, over time, Francois was able to breathe easier. Losing Alphonse was an adjustment, but in some ways, it was just as well. For months, Francois had spent most of his time back in his district in Louisiana, shoring up support and solidifying his base. The grandiose scheme and delusional vision of Richard Monroe had been a bit much for him anyway. He preferred business as usual. That might have been why he was never fully brought into Monroe's inner circle.

The passage of time would smooth everything out. Francois LaFleur knew full well the source of his own power, and it was right there in Louisiana. As long as the people kept sending him back to DC, that was enough for him—lesson learned and lesson kept.

Epilogue

Atlanta, Georgia

Acadia LaFleur sat in a wicker chair in the courtyard of the medical rehab facility in Georgia where she had been recovering for several months. The space was beautifully designed as a Japanese tea garden. A shawl covered Acadia's legs, despite the bright sunshine. She sipped tea from a china cup and basked in the warmth of the sun on her face. Acadia had surprised everyone when she suddenly awakened from her coma three months earlier. Her physical wounds were well on the way to healing. Most of the hair had grown back in the area where doctors had shaved her head to repair bone and perform surgery to relieve pressure on her brain.

The most significant remaining injury from the attack was not physical; it was memory loss. Acadia had no recall of the attack, nor could she remember anything specific since childhood. She knew who she was, but anything after the age of twelve, up to the time of the attack, was a blank.

The doctors were hopeful there might be improvement with time, but there were no guarantees. Clement II, Babette, and the grandchildren visited her weekly, bringing pictures and telling stories to try to fill in some of the gaps. Given the current residency of her husband, Alphonse, in federal prison, they'd decided to minimize his presence in the narrative for the time being. It was obvious she had been married and had children. It was also obvious that for whatever reason, her husband was no longer in the picture.

The family had decided to have Acadia continue her convalescence at the facility in Georgia. While it was a bit of a commute for her family in Alexandria, the amenities and around-the-clock staffing of the rehab center made the choice to stay a no-brainer.

Acadia placed the cup back in its saucer and smiled at her companion. She placed her hand gently on his knee, and Ben took it, wrapping his fingers around hers. A subtle electric current passed between them. He returned her smile and caressed the back of her hand. Her skin was soft, and her nails were beautifully colored and manicured.

"Thank you for spending so much time with me these past few weeks," Acadia said. "I really look forward to our time together."

"Me too," Ben replied. "You may not know it yet, but you are my best friend."

"Oh, I know it, Ben. I can tell. Were we best friends before?"

"Yes, we were," Ben replied.

"Thank you for giving me another chance."

"I'm the one who's thankful. I love you, Acadia."

"I love you too, Ben."

For more exciting adventures with Dimase Augustin, or to learn more about the author, please go to www.bruneaubooks.com